Confessions of a Kinky Wife

JUSTINE ELYOT

mischief

Mischief
An imprint of HarperCollins*Publishers*
77–85 Fulham Palace Road,
Hammersmith, London W6 8JB

www.mischiefbooks.com

A Paperback Original 2013

First published in Great Britain in ebook format by
HarperCollins*Publishers* 2013

Copyright © Justine Elyot 2013

Justine Elyot asserts the moral right to
be identified as the author of this work

A catalogue record for this book is
available from the British Library

ISBN-13: 9780007534753

Set in Sabon by FMG using Atomic ePublisher from Easypress

Find out more about HarperCollins and the environment at
www.harpercollins.co.uk/green

CONTENTS

Contents

23 June

OK, tonight's the night. It really is. It has to be.

I've lost count of the number of times I've *almost* brought the subject up.

I've rehearsed the words seventy-three times while I've cooked 'special' meals or clipped my stockings on to my suspenders or even just lain sprawled with his head in my lap watching something vaguely sexy on TV.

I always start with some kind of mention of how I'm a 'bad girl', just to see what he might say to that. But he always says, 'Just the way I like you, love,' and there we are, taking the vanilla fork in the road again, while he reaches for another handful of popcorn and pats my thigh absent-mindedly.

This makes me sound like some kind of unsatisfied horn dog but I should stress that I'm not unhappy with our sex life, and he can be prevailed upon for some slap and tickle when the mood's right and we're in the thick of things. It's always jokey and short-lived and self-conscious, though. A couple of quick swats on the bum when I bend over for rear entry, for instance, because he likes the way my cheeks jiggle. I always moan over-dramatically, encouraging more, but he must think I'm just desperate for him, because he never repeats the move.

Yeah, I know it's ironic. Communication. Exactly what I spend all day teaching troubled teenagers about. Yet, when it comes to translating my fantasies into words for my lovely husband, I'm useless.

But tonight I'm taking the bull by the horns. (Please provide your own rude joke.) Could any night be more perfect? Our third wedding anniversary. And what's your third wedding anniversary? Oh, yes – leather!

I've heard all the bawdy suggestions, thanks. Catwoman outfit, check. Strap-on, check. Gimp mask, check. None of these are what I had in mind for him, though.

I went to a little shop in town that specialised in leather goods. It was surprisingly hard to find exactly what I wanted. Everything was the wrong colour or gimmicky, over-designed with stupid monogram buckles.

What I wanted was a plain, old-fashioned man's belt, tan leather with that authentic cowhide kind of look and feel. Smooth on one side, suedey on the other, and with a big brass buckle. And the weight had to be right. I don't mean right for sitting around his hips and keeping his trousers up either. I mean right for wrapping around his fist and giving me a good thrashing with.

I browsed dozens of the wrong kind, wrinkling my nose at their unsatisfactory smell. They were too light, borderline plasticky. I needed that good, deep leather aroma that travelled like lightning from my nostrils to my clit.

When I found it, I had to take a moment, look over my shoulder to make sure nobody saw me, and breathe deep and long.

Oh, yes. That was the one. Right colour, right weight, right buckle, right feel, right smell. This was the belt my husband could whip me with.

I felt ridiculously coy taking it to the counter. I had to keep telling myself that it's perfectly usual for a man to receive a belt as a present and nobody's going to assume I'm a pervert. But I just felt that the man who untagged it and wrapped it and took my money knew perfectly well what I wanted it for. And he thought I deserved it too.

By the time I left the shop, I was in a stew of arousal. I walked to the car with wet knickers and nipples punching their way out of my bra cups. When I got home, I took the belt out of its bag and lay on the sofa, sniffing it, while I slipped my hands inside my knickers.

I fantasised about Dan coming home early and catching

me at it. In my fantasy he was still wearing his uniform, even though he has to change at the end of each shift in real life, and he strode over, snatched the belt off me and ordered me over the back of the sofa.

'What have I told you about that?' he said sternly, pulling my knickers down to my knees. 'You don't do it without me. You don't come when I'm not around. Is that so hard to understand?'

'No, Sir.'

'So why can't you behave yourself?'

'I guess I'm a bad girl, Sir.'

'Yes. And you know what happens to bad girls.'

He was wrapping the buckle end around his fist.

'Yes, Sir.'

'What?'

He trailed the V-shaped end over my bare bum cheeks, cold and ticklish.

'They get punished, Sir.'

'That's right. You're going to learn your lesson, Pip. It's going to be a hard one, but that's what you need.'

That's what I need. Oh, yes.

He was only halfway through the spanking, the leather falling full-strength, heating my arse like fire, before I came, really hard. I jerked around so much that the belt slid off my face and on to the carpet.

No sign of Dan, though. Hardly surprising because his shift didn't finish till nine.

My orgasm had ironed out the knots a tough day's work had added to my spine, though, so it was all good. I headed for the shower and thought, yet again, about how I was going to talk him into what I had in mind.

So, anyway, wedding anniversary. Tonight's the night and I've got champagne on ice for when we get home from the restaurant. I've also got the dark red silk underwear on underneath this dress. I'm waiting for him to change into his best suit and then we're off out. The Talk will happen. Wish me luck.

24 June

It was a lovely night, amazing food and the most romantic setting, overlooking the river, but the restaurant was a little ... intimate. By which I mean that it was very difficult not to overhear the conversations taking place at other tables.

This made me nervous, and so did Dan, because he looked so bloody gorgeous. He had on the dark suit he wore to my sister's wedding and he knows I can't resist him in that. He knows because he got to shag me up against the register office back wall while the groom's family photographs were being taken on the front steps. He looked utterly, unbelievably, mouth-wateringly sexy, with his two top shirt buttons undone, so a little chest hair tantalised the eye.

Dan looks good in everything, mind you, whether he's patrolling the streets in his uniform or mowing the lawn in ripped jeans and a tight T-shirt. He makes my tongue hang out. I have to keep remembering to put it away. He's tall and dark and all the running after criminals keeps him fit. He has a face that can do anything, as well. I've seen him go from boyish twinkle to roguish glint to 100 per cent wicked in the time it takes to raise an eyebrow.

I remember how he bowled me over the first time we met. I sat there on that orange moulded plastic chair, watching him in a trance. I'm not sure I breathed once in the twenty minutes it took for him to question and charge the kid I was acting as Appropriate Adult for. The only thought in my mind was Who? Is? That?

Obviously I stayed professional, much as I was dying to play footsie under the battered, cigarette-burnt old desk. The way he flicked his eyes over me from time to time made me think there might be a little bit of something similar going on with him too.

When I left the station, he caught me on the steps, all breathless and tousled. God, I wanted to wrestle him to the floor then and there. I restrained myself, what with being in the company of a furious fifteen-year-old, and simply nodded and smiled while he volunteered to give a talk on police/community relations at my Vulnerable Young People's group.

I think I actually said, 'Awesome!'

The fifteen-year-old teased me about it all the way back to the children's home.

'He wants you, Pip. Better watch out if you don't want Plod in yer knickers.'

I blanked this line of conversation, but inside I wanted to hear more.

He came and did the talk to a group who started out hostile and ended up charmed and positive. He has the knack of making people want him to like them, so that they strive to please him. It's a neat trick – I wish I had it.

Anyway, he'd won them over, so just imagine how I felt. He'd seduced me already – the physical side of it was a mere formality. We sat in my office after locking up the building and shared a bottle of wine and talked very earnestly about the social issues affecting my Vulnerable Young People until the switch flipped and every single thing we said seemed to be a form of verbal foreplay.

We kissed against my filing cabinet and ended up at my flat. I don't think we've spent a night apart since, shift patterns permitting.

And now here we are, three years married, and he's still the funniest, sweetest, kindest, most capable and sexy and sometimes slightly annoying but not that much man in the world.

So why the hell was I contemplating asking him for more?

In the low-voiced, elegant atmosphere of the restaurant, I panicked. I couldn't go through with it. What if I scared him? Why would I risk my marriage to this man?

The first thing he said on sitting down was 'I've got a little something for you.' And he rustled a package inside a shopping bag.

'Can't we ... do the presents at home?'

'But you've brought mine.' He looked puzzled. I love his puzzled face. Just adorable.

'I know, I just ... it's a bit ... it's not very *private* here, is it?'

'Oh.' His eyes lit up. '*That* kind of present, eh?'

Fuck. Now he was expecting something from a sex shop. Oh, God. I wanted to bolt from the restaurant, take the belt back to the shop and exchange it, quickety-quick, for a lacy basque and a set of nipple tassels.

'Don't get your hopes up,' I said.

'It's my wedding anniversary,' he said. 'If I can't get my hopes up on my wedding anniversary, when *can* I get them up?'

'Good point,' I said, then, suddenly inspired, 'So, what are your hopes?'

What if I could bring him to confess his own hidden desire for kink? What if he longed to redden my bottom but was just too worried it would appal me?

9

'For tonight?'

He was about to lean over the table and murmur into my ear, but the waiter appeared with our champagne cocktails and menus, so the moment was lost.

'I really want to give you your present,' he said, sipping and watching me.

'I don't mind waiting.'

'I know *you* don't. But I want to give you it now. I've been looking forward to it.'

'Oh ...' I looked around. Everybody seemed pretty involved with their own conversations. 'Go on, then.'

He beamed and handed over his bag, then retreated into his champagne glass, sipping with measured calm.

I opened the delicate tissue wrapping and had to clap a hand over my mouth to stop myself screaming.

'Happy anniversary, my darling little Twinkletoes,' he said, flushing with pleasure at my reaction.

'Is this genuine?'

'It's not a bloody knock-off. What do you take me for?'

'A genuine Mulberry Alexa? Christ, Dan, these cost a fortune.'

'Well, I got it from an outlet store,' he said. 'It wasn't that bad.'

'I don't know what to say.' I turned the deliciously soft tan leather every which way, putting it up to my face and sniffing, just the way I did with the belt. It was the most beautiful thing I'd ever been given.

10

He was perfect. Why would I want to change him? I felt guilty and cheap for even considering it.

'You don't have to say anything. It's written all over your face.'

He sat back and basked, while I became conscious of the indulgent good wishes of the other diners. Suddenly the parcel at my feet became my nemesis, a terrible mistake. I should have got him something else.

Too late.

'So, come on then. Hand it over.'

He held out a palm. Lately, he couldn't do that without me imagining how it would feel cracking down on my bum. Tonight was no different.

I shut my eyes for a second of unspoken prayer, then reached down for the gift.

The shop had been a high-end establishment and they had put the belt in a smart silk-lined box with a gold monogram. When Dan unwrapped it, I think he was expecting something you'd find in a jeweller's, like cufflinks or a watch.

He looked surprised when he opened the box.

'Oh,' he said, pulling it out. It was rolled up like a coiled snake, a deadly spiral in his hand. 'This is a very de luxe number, isn't it?'

'Do you like it? I just thought it would look really good on you.'

Suddenly I was desperate that he didn't guess my true

11

intention. I wanted to turn back that tide, ignore my stupid repressed fantasies and live with what I had.

'It looks vintage,' he said.

God, he had uncoiled it and was letting it slide around his palm, then he pulled it taut between his hands and I nearly doubled over with arousal.

Surely he must see the effect this had on me? Instant wetness, so much so that I worried about leaving a damp patch on the chair.

'It's pretty sexy,' I said.

He gave me a crooked smile. 'You think?'

Waiter-with-chronic-bad-timing appeared to take our order and the sexual vibe lowered to a simmer, but it was nonetheless there all the way through the three courses, especially since the belt lay on the white table-cloth for all to see.

I imagined that everyone knew what it was *really* for.

Everyone knew that it had been left there, in my line of sight, to remind me what awaited me after the meal. They were all aware that, once the last mouthful of dessert had been swallowed, I was going to be escorted out through the kitchen to the back yard, bent over a barrel with my dress up and knickers down and strapped long and hard by my elegantly besuited husband.

What for? I tried to make up a reason, but I was fatally distracted by my own lust and the growing excitement in the pit of my stomach. It made for an uncomfortable eating experience, but three courses were a challenge for me anyway, so I picked and pecked at my food.

'Aren't you going to eat that?'

Dan, his appetite as reliably healthy as always, plucked a tuile biscuit from my plate and bit into it.

Some of the other diners had left the restaurant now, and we had a little more latitude for un-eavesdropped conversation.

I stroked the edge of the belt with one finger and said, 'Do you really like it?'

'Of course.'

'I've wanted to get you one just like it for ages.'

He just held his smile, expectant, waiting for me to elaborate.

'I think it would feel nice,' I said hesitantly. Oh shit, now it was coming out. Could I take that back?

'Feel nice?' he said.

I stared down at the melted ice cream on my plate, too mortified to continue.

'You've gone bright red,' he said, but his smile slowly widened. 'OK, I think it's time to get the bill and get the hell out of here. Things just got interesting.'

The restaurant was a short distance from our flat by the harbour. Dan walked me back with one hand around my elbow, the new belt wrapped around his other set of knuckles. Damn, it looked good there. Man and belt in living harmony. I was wildly optimistic as we headed into the lift and, as was our tradition, snogged all the way up to the third floor.

We tipped ourselves out and fumbled the key in the lock and somehow didn't collapse on the hall floor. Instead we made a kissing, grabbing, lunging progress into the living room and managed to stay upright all the way over to the sofa.

He pinned me to it and I felt that soft leather brush my wrist.

'So, then, Pip,' he said, his wide white grin inches from mine. 'Tell me what you meant when you said my belt would *feel* nice. Because, as far as I'm aware, belts are meant to keep trousers up. How could that make you feel nice? Hmm?'

'I just thought … you know … it's so soft and it smells so good …'

'Don't. I know what you thought.'

'Do you?'

My heart jumped high, sealing up my throat so I could barely breathe.

'Fancy a bit of slap and tickle, do we?'

I giggled, writhing happily underneath him. Yes! This could happen. This was starting to happen.

'Maybe more slap than tickle,' I whispered.

'Are you sure?'

'Do I have to sign a consent form?'

'Story of my life. Paperwork, paperwork, paperwork. But no. I think in this case a verbal agreement holds good. Go on then. Turn over.'

He let go of my wrists and knelt up, watching me flip myself on to my stomach. My face rested against a velvet cushion, handy if I needed anything to yell into. We didn't want to disturb the neighbours, after all.

I felt the tickly swish of my skirt being raised. It was a shame I had to imagine the look on his face as he uncovered lacy briefs and matching suspenders and stockings, but I'd seen it often enough before and at least I got to hear his low sigh of pleasure.

Rather than any sharp and sudden smack, the next physical contact was his lips on the low curve of my bottom, kissing their way over every inch of the flesh my knickers weren't protecting. This kindled an amazing tingle, flooding my pussy and making my skin supersensitive until I began to rather dread what I'd asked for.

Could I take it back and just carry on with this instead?

His fingers slipped inside the lacy elastic of my knickers, then down the suspender straps, pulling them out and letting them snap back so that I squealed.

'Thought you'd like that,' he said, his hands between my thighs now, pulling them apart. 'Since you're into pain these days.'

'It's not that I'm into pain,' I said, my voice muffled by the cushion.

15

'No? What then?'

'Just … the whole idea turns me on, that's all.'

'The whole idea?'

'Yeah. Being, I dunno, taken in hand. Dominated.'

'Oh, so it's a headspace thing.'

'Totally.'

'And I'm in charge, am I?'

'If you want to be.'

'So what if I just want to order you to get on your knees and suck me off?'

I huffed. I hoped he wasn't going to miss the point now.

'If you want to do that, do it. But it's about both of us getting what we want, not just one of us.'

'Right. And what you want is a good, sound spanking, is it?'

Oh, just hearing the words, spoken by him in his 'arresting officer' voice, could have got me off then and there.

'Mmm, oh, God, yeah.'

'Well,' he said, his fingertips grazing the crotch of my knickers, stroking it up and down, up and down until my hips were undulating in sympathetic rhythm. 'I'm not sure what you've done to deserve it. Apart from buy me a lovely anniversary present and give me three terrific years of marriage but … let's say that you're in trouble for having a bum that stops traffic.'

16

I snorted and tried to kick my legs but, as he was kneeling on them, that didn't make much difference.

'Oh, yes, you stand accused of conducting your arse without due care and attention, so that everyone on the public highway was distracted by it. How do you plead?'

'Guilty,' I proclaimed, steeling myself for the first blow.

It was much lighter than I anticipated, a little exploratory slap, so flimsy and weak-wristed I twisted my neck and frowned at him.

'That's it?'

'Thing is, love,' he said, his face crumpled in apology. 'I'm not sure I can hurt you. Do you really want me to make it sting?'

'Don't hold back,' I urged him. 'I'll tell you if it's too much, I promise.'

'Well, OK.' He tried again, and this one made a most satisfying echo, his hand falling quite heavily across the meat of my right cheek. Oh, it hurt, but not too much. Really, just enough. I wondered how much it would take to get my arse really bright red, because that was what I wanted. No half-hearted blush pink, or rapidly fading warmth. I needed the full effect.

'Harder,' I said. 'I've been bad.'

'Have you now?' More deliberate, forceful smacks landed on my rear. 'You'll have to tell me all about that. What have you done?'

'I had bad thoughts,' I gasped, starting to feel the burn

spread through my lower body. 'When you were on night shift, I thought about things you could do to me. All the time. And it made me touch myself.'

'Oh, you naughty thing,' he tutted, spanking steadily. 'Perhaps we should have a rule. No touching, except by me. What do you think?'

'Yes, yes.' I grasped on to this eagerly. I had often fantasised about being punished for masturbating.

'So we have a genuine rule break to address,' he said. 'I think that calls for no knickers, don't you?'

He paused and pulled the stretchy lace down to my stocking tops, baring my now rather warm bottom.

'You're wet,' he said, crouching to inspect my exposed pussy. He prodded at the lips, holding them aside for a better view of the hidden guilty secrets. One long finger glided easily up inside me. 'Very wet,' he amended. 'Not much of a punishment, is it, if it's turning you on?'

'I can't help it,' I protested. 'My body does it for me.'

'Perhaps we'll have to think of something else. Something you really won't enjoy. A nice big pile of washing up, maybe.'

'Perhaps you'll just have to spank harder,' I prompted. This wasn't funny, no matter what he thought, chuckling away up there with his finger shoved inside me.

'Well, it's worth a try, I suppose.'

He emptied my pussy and reverted to heating up my arse, but this time his technique was different, much

18

faster and less predictable. It was infinitely more difficult to take and I was quick to squirm and yelp and try to pull my legs out from under him. He was having none of it, though, and he held me down, his fist in the small of my back like a human paperweight.

'Feeling it now, are you?'

'That. Really. Hurts,' I complained, jerking my hips as best I could.

'Do you want me to stop?'

I shook my head. The heat was building beautifully and I didn't want to call time until my skin was tight with it.

'Good,' he said. 'I wasn't sure about this to begin with, but I think I like it now. I think I could take to this.'

I stuffed the cushion into my mouth, suppressing a howl as he laid a particularly wicked volley on both cheeks.

Be careful what you wish for.

'Your arse looks gorgeous, all lit up and glowing,' he gloated. 'I think you might have created a monster, love. And we haven't even got to the belt yet.'

'Ow,' I said. It seemed to encapsulate my emotions.

'OK, let's temper justice with mercy, shall we? I think that'll do for your first time. Now.' He put his forearm under my stomach and encouraged me gently on to my knees, with my face still buried in the cushion.

I heard the business of trousers being unzipped, fabric falling behind me.

19

'Poor little pickle,' he crooned.

I felt the tip of his cock butting into my juices.

'God, you are so wet!' he exclaimed, obviously impressed. 'This'll be like a knife going into butter.'

And it was. An exceptionally blunt, thick knife, right into my slippery slick butter dish, so to speak. I couldn't get enough of him, pushing myself back on to him, especially when he rammed himself right up against my hot cheeks. He held my hips tight and I felt taken, owned, mastered. God, it was the hottest thing ever. When I came I bit into the cushion to stop myself screaming.

Afterwards, lying on the sofa all rumpled and hot and tired, he picked the belt up off the floor.

'Didn't even get to use this,' he said, yawning. 'But it's coming to you. Happy Anniversary, love.'

I can't wait.

15 July

We've had a busy few weeks, lots of overtime for Dan, and I've been trying to put together some summer-holiday workshops for my adolescents. Some additional family stress surrounding my mother-in-law (who else?) has also been ongoing, taking our attention away from our marriage and sex life to an extent.

We've fooled about a bit, but any kinky stuff has been spur-of-the-moment and limited to a few smacks with the wooden spoon while I'm making dinner or whatever.

And, while I like the fun aspect of it, and can't complain at how it seems to have pepped up our bedroom activities, I can't help craving something a little *more*. Do I mean more? Or do I mean different? I don't know.

The thing is, I'm not good with stress. In my day job, I have to model absolute patience and absolute tolerance, but this has always made Dan laugh because he knows that I'm actually extremely *im*patient and *in*tolerant a lot of the time. I nearly ruined our relationship in the first year of marriage by constantly blowing my stack over the slightest little thing. I kept blaming him for everything – if I couldn't find the scissors, *he* must have put them in the wrong place, though half the time it was me who'd done it.

I did this so often that we ended up having a blazing row that must have kept the neighbours awake, with him threatening to move into the section house. Since then, I've tried to work on my temper, but I'm not sure my strategy of passive-aggressive stomping around and silent moodiness is really the best one.

Ever since he spanked me on our wedding anniversary, I've had this mad fantasy about him doing it as a genuine punishment. Not in an overbearing, patriarchal sort of way, but from a desire to help me overcome my faults and be a better person. Loving discipline, if that makes any sense at all. I'm tired of feeling guilty about my outbursts, or simmering and keeping all the resentment and irritation inside me. Perhaps, if he spanked it out of me, I'd be able to address my petty annoyances with openness and honesty, like a proper adult. Not that I've ever felt like a proper adult. Does anyone, ever? I constantly feel that events are spiralling out of my control and I want someone to take that control for me. I want it to be him.

But I'm afraid to broach the subject with him. I think he'll feel weird about it. So I've kept it to myself so far.

I've ordered a book, though. *The Guiding Hand – A Disciplinary Manual for Loving Husbands.* Sounds like some kind of crackpot 50s-throwback thing, doesn't it? But the blurb alone turned me on so much I had to order it.

17 July

So my new book arrived and it's fascinating. I can't stop reading it.

I mean, I fundamentally disagree with nearly all of what the author thinks about male and female roles; a lot of it's horrifically sexist, not to mention homophobic, but if you pretend it's a manual for any dominant person and their lover – instead of traditional heterosexual married couples – it starts to make a bit of sense.

I would die if anyone caught me with it but I just can't put it down. I'm so conflicted, it's as if I have an even split down the middle of me. There's Pip the right-on youth worker and Pip the submissive wifey. Oh, God, I really can't do this.

I'm going to have to put the book away and forget about it.

It's just a fantasy.

That's all.

20 *July*

Oh, bugger.

Dan has found the book.

Everything had been going so well, too. We had the best night last night, and he actually used his new belt on me.

We went out for drinks with friends and were both in a very happy, high, flirty mood all evening. I couldn't help teasing him and making cheeky little remarks and there came a moment, halfway through the final drink, when he leaned into me and said, right into my ear, 'My belt's coming out when I get you home, missy.'

It was ridiculously exciting. I bit my lip and clenched everything in my effort not to squeal. I made puppy-dog eyes at him, as if begging him to reconsider, but I had to tone it down a bit in case people cottoned on.

He laughed and squeezed my knee and said no more about it, but the promise was so heavy in the air that I could barely swallow the last inch of my wine and longed for all the goodbyes to be over with, quickly, so we could get home.

As soon as we were through the door, he had me up against the hall wall, his hand braced above my head, his forehead almost touching mine.

'Someone's been begging for a belting,' he said softly. 'Haven't they?'

'I don't know what you mean,' I said, coyly over-dramatic, the situation making my face burn.

'Yes, you do, you minx.'

He held me by my chin and took a fierce kiss from me until I nearly lost the use of my legs and slid down the wall like a person in a cartoon.

'Go on,' he said, releasing me. 'Get those jeans down and bend over the arm of the sofa.'

I stared at him, joyously open-mouthed.

'Now!' he ordered.

I scampered off at the double, and, shivering inside, unbuttoned and lowered the jeans. Once they were mussed around my ankles, I bent over the arm of the chair, presenting my bottom in its sensible M&S cotton knickers.

'That's it,' he said approvingly, once he had come out of the bedroom with the belt. 'You know you need it, don't you?'

27

'Oh,' I lamented, not quite able to talk the submissive talk, good as I was at bending over.

'No, come on, I asked you a question, love. Now, what's the answer? Do you need it, or do you need it?'

I snorted. 'Both.'

'Good. Right, I think these might be surplus to requirements.'

He pulled the knickers down.

'You should have told me to take them off,' I said, mildly surprised.

'Are you telling me what to do? As it happens, I like pulling them down. It gives me a nice feeling. Right here.'

He nudged his jean-clad crotch into the lower curve of my bottom. It was hard already. When he pressed it into my pussy, he soaked it in my flowing juices.

'Point taken,' I said.

'Now get that arse nice and high, ready to be kissed by the leather. More than kissed, I'd say. A good, long, full-on snog with tongues.'

'Oh, bloody hell,' I said, nervous now. What if it was unbearably painful?

He paused and put a hand on my bottom.

'You OK?'

I nodded vigorously.

'Fine, honestly. Just a little … apprehensive.'

'Yeah, well, you'll tell me to stop if it gets too much, right?'

'Go back to being all mean and dominant, Dan. I'll tell you, I promise.'

'Right you are. Mean and dominant.'

He put his fist underneath my nose. It had the belt partly wrapped around it, about half of its length trailing away over the side of the sofa.

I took a good deep sniff and my eyes crossed with heavenly lust.

'You're getting that,' he told me. 'Kiss it. Go on.'

I laid my lips reverently on the supple hide, then watched it disappear from view.

I tensed my buttocks, but all that happened was a light, ticklish sensation as the V-shaped end of the belt dangled between my cheeks.

I twitched.

'That tickles.'

'It'll tickle you some more. Stop tensing up.'

He patted my rump until I unknotted the muscles, cursing him under my breath.

I didn't hear the belt fly through the air – I'd been hoping for that sexy whipping sound – so when it landed on my bum I was a bit shocked and my hand flew behind me to cover the little patch of sting it had left there.

'Move your hand,' commanded Dan, then, when I didn't, he grabbed my wrist and tucked it under my stomach where it rested on the sofa arm. 'No more of that or I'll give you double strokes.'

I waited for the second, and then tried to work out if it was more or less painful than his hand. His hand was heavier and covered more area, but this had a unique viperish quality to it that promised torments to come.

It was deceptive in its lightness, little whispers of pain flicking over my bottom until he started to lay it on more heavily and then I began to rock and gasp. Solid bars of heat fell, one, two, three, then stopped.

I looked over my shoulder. He had put the belt down. Was that it?

'No,' he said, in answer to the unspoken question. 'Just an interlude.'

He spread my thighs and began to rub my clit, gently, not enough to bring me off, but little teasing touches that had me pushing myself on his fingers and moaning for more.

'Just as wet as ever,' he said. 'You want it, don't you? God, you're horny as fuck. Sorry, Twink.'

He took his fingers away and I pouted.

'I'm not finished yet.'

The belt lashed down again and now it made a loud crack every time. I hoped our thin walls were enough to keep the noise from disturbing the neighbours. What on earth would they think we were doing? Would it be obvious? The thought that they knew Dan was giving my arse a good thrashing with his belt got me through six more hard strokes, keeping me soaking wet and ready.

He put the belt down again, just as I was starting to struggle. My breath staggered out in uneven pants and I prepared for more fingering, hoping he would press a bit harder this time.

But no.

It was his tongue, warm and wet, that pushed at my pussy next. He made a seal with his lips around my clit and breathed on it until it felt so hot and swollen I had to wriggle my hips furiously. Then the very tip of his tongue flicked at it, so tantalisingly I wanted to sob.

'Oh, fuck, please,' I wheedled. 'Oh, yes.'

But he wouldn't give me the pressure I craved. It was like having a feather lightly brushed over my clit, his devilishly unsatisfying combination of breaths and little tongue-tickles. I began to wish he'd get back to strapping me instead.

And so he did, six more firm strokes, and the harder he did it, the more I seemed able to take.

When he dropped the belt again, I was straining and beginning to sweat, but a strange kind of exhilaration made me want more.

Instead, Dan pushed the first couple of inches inside me and held it there until I begged him to fuck me.

'Do you think you deserve it?' he said.

'I deserve it. I'm a bad girl.'

'Then that means you need more of my belt, doesn't it?'

'Ohhh.' I was delighted, loving every thrust, every stern word that went with it, even though it was more of his cock I really craved.

Obligingly, he pushed further in, but still with a maddening slowness that made me jolt my hips backwards, trying to catch his full length.

Once he was all the way in, I sighed deeply, ready for pleasure. But he thrust three times, then withdrew, and I was still vocalising my outrage when the belt lashed down again.

'Just to make sure the message is getting through,' he said, putting his shoulder into six more strokes.

I was struggling now, and he seemed to know it. When he put the belt down, I was right on the verge of tears and pleas. I drew a huge breath of relief and spread my thighs in invitation.

But, once he was inside me, giving me the hard fucking I'd wanted all along, part of me wished he hadn't stopped. Part of me wished he'd carried on whipping my bum until the tears came and the pleas rained down, and then he'd whipped right through them. Did that make me wrong in the head?

I imagined him doing this while he powered into me from behind, imagined my bottom even sorer, my submission absolute. In the end it was those thoughts, rather than his stout attentions to my pussy, that made me come.

'I need this,' I sighed, while he speeded up and got ready to fill me with his spunk. 'I need it.'

He grabbed my shoulder so hard it nearly dislocated, his orgasm mightier than usual, then lay down beside me, beaded with sweat, his eyes wide with astonishment at what had just overtaken him.

'I know,' he said. 'I see. I know.'

It was a lovely afterglow and he seemed so happy to have found his kinky side and had some fun with it.

But I don't think his reaction to the book will be good. I think that will change the game completely.

21 July

He waited until after dinner to bring the subject up. Of course, I couldn't eat. I was too busy trying to second-guess his reaction, but he was playing things totally straight, being normal Dan, full of stories about his colleagues and complaints about form-filling.

I was washing up in the kitchen when he wandered in, picked up a tea towel as if preparing to dry, and flicked it at my bottom, making me jump and rub at it.

'Oi!' I said.

'What? You like that, don't you?'

'Not always. Not when I'm not expecting it.'

'Oh, so it's you calling the shots, is it?' He stood behind me and clasped his arms around me, holding me there with his chin on top of my head. 'Funny, that.'

'Why funny?' I asked guardedly.

'I thought you were into that whole submissive thing these days.'

I twisted my neck round to look at his eyes. His face was quite grave.

'You saw that book,' I said.

'Yeah, I did. You can't seriously tell me that, after everything you say and do at work, day after day, you believe all that guff about fixed gender roles and male and female energies?'

'No, Jesus, no, I don't!'

'Well, thank fuck for that. I thought a tornado had taken our flat and transplanted it in Stepford.'

I shook my head. 'I believe the same things I've always believed.'

'That's what I thought. You like a bit of kink in the bedroom but you're still the same person ... this book is a bit weird, though. I can't figure it out.'

I took a deep breath.

'Look, Dan. The thing is, I like kink. I like to be spanked for fun. But ... I think I want something a bit more than that too.' I put my hand in the washing-up water, which was far too hot, and withdrew it rapidly.

'Put the Marigolds on,' he said.

I made a face. I hated putting the Marigolds on. They made my hands smell fusty for hours afterwards.

'I'll be all right,' I said, tipping a handful of cutlery into the bubbles.

'You'll scald yourself. Put them on.'

I ignored him, picked up the cloth, plunged my hands quickly into the water and gasped as I withdrew a fork.

'Jesus, Pip, why? Your hand looks like it's been skinned. I can't watch.'

He let go of me and took a step back.

He was right. That water was boiling and my hand throbbed so much I could barely hold the fork. I put it under a stream of cold water, exhaling with sweet relief.

When the burning was soothed, I turned around and leant against the sink, facing him.

'That sums it up,' I said. 'That's what I mean.'

'What?'

'You're so sensible, Dan, and so capable, and I'm not. I do things like that all the time, and I get frustrated with myself and then I get angry with myself and then … I don't know. It just boils away in my brain, a great big swamp of self-loathing that keeps getting added to and added to. It's not good for me.'

'It's no big deal, love. Just a silly mistake. Don't be so hard on yourself.'

'Exactly. I don't want to be hard on myself. I want *you* to be hard on me.'

My heart pounded, and the palm that had been hot and itchy from the scalding water was now sweating.

'Like the guys in your book, you mean? You want me to actually … discipline you?'

I nodded vigorously.

'I want to be held to account. I want to be corrected.'

He laughed, a tad nervously, and looked up at the ceiling.

'I'm sorry, Pip, I don't mean to laugh at you. It's just … uh … unusual. Isn't it? I've spent my whole life trying to be respectful of women, you know …'

'It's not about you being a man and me being a woman. It's nothing to do with that at all. It's to do with me wanting to submit and having this need. Oh, I don't know if I'm putting it very well.'

'So if I wanted you to spank me, that would be fine?'

'Well, I'd find it hard, because I don't like dominating, but in principle, yes.'

'Right. I don't, by the way. Want you spank me, I mean. I'm not that way inclined.'

He tried a smile. I tried one back. It was encouraging, at least, that he hadn't walked out of the door with words of a 'no dice' variety.

'I'm not asking you to do anything you don't want to,' I said. 'It's just a thought. Just a thing I've been pondering. I wanted to find out a bit more about it so I got a book. I'm not demanding anything of you.'

'You're not?'

'No. God, Dan, I'm happy with you. I love you. I

don't want you to change and I'm not some unsatisfied wife eaten up by sexual frustration. Far from it. But I think, for me, this discipline thing would work so well … it's just a thought. That's all.'

'You have some interesting thoughts, don't you, Twink?' he said. 'Now put those flaming Marigolds on, for Christ's sake.'

And there the matter ended. (I did put the gloves on.)

25 July

This has been the hardest working week in recent memory. Two of my kids have been in trouble with the law while another took an overdose. I spent all of last night in A&E with her, lobbying furiously to get her a place in an adolescent mental health unit. We got a bed in the end, but I feel like I've fought through every one of the seven labours of Hercules.

Then I've been at work all day, having to write reports. School holidays have started so the kids are kicking their heels, hanging around the centre demanding to be stimulated and fed and all the rest. I felt guilty about neglecting them to get the reports done, but I have a looming deadline and just had to leave them to play table-tennis and mess around on the DJ decks while I sat in the office with the door wedged open. Luckily Grant, my student assistant, turned up mid-afternoon and was able to keep more of an eye on them.

He offered to run the evening session to give me a break, but I feel like I should be there. There are some volatile relationships, especially among the older boys, and I worry that something will kick off in my absence.

So I nipped off at five, visited Jessie in the mental health unit (she seemed quite calm) and went home to grab a quick bite to eat before going back for the evening session.

'You're going back?' Dan wasn't exactly thrilled to hear it. 'You look dead on your feet, love. Can't someone else do it? Reva?'

'She's on holiday.'

I was too tired to even think about what I wanted to eat and just sank down on a dining chair, my head spinning.

'What about that student bloke? Student Grant?'

'Oh, he's not experienced enough.'

'I thought you said he used to be in the army and he's thirty-eight years old.'

'Yeah, but square-bashing and teen wrangling aren't exactly the same thing ...'

'Whatever. He's more than capable of overseeing a bit of disco dancing. Go on, call him and see if he's free.'

'He is. He offered to do it but ...'

'Well, there you are then. Problem solved. Call him.'

'I'll just worry …'

Dan snatched the phone from its cradle and thrust it at me.

'Do it,' he said. 'And then you're going to bed.'

Oh, God. I suddenly realised. He was doing what I'd hinted I wanted him to do. He was taking control when I wasn't able to do it for myself. But now he was doing it, I wasn't sure I wanted him to! I just wanted to whine and make excuses and argue him into giving in. But then I would get a horrible evening trying to run a teen disco on no hours' sleep while he stewed here, feeling pissed off and unlistened to.

When it came down to it, he was right.

'OK,' I said, and with that I was liberated. Everything was taken off my shoulders and I could float into deep peace and relaxation.

I called Grant, who readily agreed to run the disco. He would have helped out anyway, having seen how pale and lacklustre I'd been earlier. He thought I needed a night off.

'Have you been talking to my husband?' I asked, suspicious, but he just laughed and said he'd see me tomorrow.

Dan smiled encouragingly at me as I hit the 'end call' button.

'See. Not that hard, was it? What do you want to eat? What did you have for lunch?'

41

'Oh.' I thought vaguely about the lunch hour, then remembered that I'd worked right through it, with some half-formed intention of popping across to the little newsagent over the road later and getting a plastic-wrapped sandwich. Later had never come around. 'I forgot.'

The look he gave me made me bite my lip. It would have turned me on if I hadn't been too tired to even remember what sex was. As it went, I just hung my head and said, 'I meant to, but I had reports ...'

'We talked about this before, didn't we?' he said. 'After you fainted that time. I seem to remember you promising me you'd take better care of yourself.'

'It was just this once,' I said, but then I remembered that that was a lie. 'A few times,' I amended. 'Not often. Look, I get busy, you know I do.' My tone had switched from sheepish to querulous. It wasn't fair that I should be in trouble for working too hard.

Despite the fact that I fantasised about Dan taking control in this way, now he was doing it, I felt my long-buried rebellious schoolgirl making her presence known. It seemed like the default response – sniping and arguing.

I wanted him to stand firm, and yet I also wanted to win.

It was all too confusing and, in the end, my tiredness made the decision for me.

'We're going to discuss that in the morning,' he said. 'But for now – bed. Go on. No arguments. I'll bring you some supper on a tray.'

I nodded, my eyes half-shut already, and drifted across the kitchen. He caught me halfway and held me close, kissing me goodnight. I wanted to sleep there, in his arms, but he sent me on my way with a pat on my bottom.

I think it could be a taste of things to come.

26 July

Be careful what you wish for.

Great advice, but impossible to follow. Wishes come unbidden and desires can't be quelled. I wished for it, I got it. I really, really got it.

I was woken with a kiss.

'Sleeping beauty,' he said.

The room was still dark and my alarm hadn't gone off.

'Wass time?' I tried to come to, but everything was blurred and the bed felt like a place I wanted to stay in for a lot longer.

'Early,' he said. 'I thought we'd get up an hour earlier. We've both got work today, and I want to sort a few things out while they're still fresh in our minds.'

Something about the way he said the words sent a warning pang right down to my solar plexus. Actually, it went a bit lower than that. I squinted at him through one eye.

He was sitting up in bed, looking ahead, his face perfectly grave. When he caught my glance, he raised an eyebrow, unsmiling.

If he was playing a role, he was doing it very convincingly.

I was scared of him. Actually scared.

But it was exhilarating at the same time.

'You mean … about last night?' I said.

'Yes, I do. We have issues to address, Pip. Go and shower and brush your teeth and whatnot and then I want you straight back in here in your pyjamas. Understood?'

I think he wanted me to say, 'Yes, Sir' but I didn't give him that satisfaction. Instead, I said, 'Are you serious?'

'Do I look like I'm joking, Philippa?'

Oh, bloody hell, *Philippa*.

It was enough to send me out of bed and into the bathroom without another word.

Under the hot shower jets I woke up properly, the citrusy scent of my shampoo acting like a stimulant to my senses. I put my hand on my bottom and felt the water stream over it. What sort of state might that be in by the time he was finished with me?

I pressed my thighs together and squirmed, feeling hot and breathless at the thought. I was going to be punished. Actually punished for my bad behaviour, and I had never looked forward to anything more. I didn't care how much it was going to hurt – I hoped it would hurt a lot and I'd have to beg him to stop.

I washed myself carefully, getting every inch of myself as fresh and soft as I could, paying special attention to my bum. I wanted it to look good over his lap, or wherever he was going to put me. If the poor man had to do this terrible thing to me, the least he deserved was a nice view.

I towelled myself dry, scrubbed my teeth and put my pyjamas back on. They were thin cotton summer pyjamas – just plain white shorts and a vest. The material wouldn't offer much protection, even if I was allowed to keep them on.

Allowed. The word made me cross my arms over my chest and shiver. I was going to be subject to Dan's authority. Whatever he said in the next hour went. I wondered how naturally obedience would come to me.

Only one way to find out.

I stood dithering by the door handle for so long that he called out to ask if everything was all right in there.

His voice galvanised me and I walked into the bedroom, in pyjamas and hair wrapped in a towel turban.

'You'll have to dry your hair,' he said. 'I'll get a shower while you're sorting yourself out.'

While I sat at the dressing table, drying and straightening my hair, I looked into the mirror and noticed a few things. He had made the bed, but he'd put my pillows out in the centre of the duvet, one on top of the other.

Next to them, laid out neatly, were The Belt and my wooden-backed hairbrush.

'Oh.' I moaned out loud.

This was actually happening. I didn't know whether to squeal or swear.

My hair was dry before Dan came out of the shower. I wasn't sure what to do, but I didn't dare approach the bed with its frightful accessories, so I simply sat quietly at the dressing table, rather compulsively arranging my nail polishes into colour groups.

When he came out, I couldn't look at him, but I caught sight in the mirror of his smart dark trousers and white shirt. A wave of synthetic ocean freshness blasted my nostrils when he came closer and crouched down behind me, looking at my face in the mirror over my shoulder.

'All ready?' he whispered, putting his hands over my bare upper arms.

'I don't know,' I whispered back. 'Depends what I have to be ready for.'

'Go and sit down on the edge of the bed,' he said.

I obeyed without thinking, sinking my bottom down into the comfort of the duvet. He took a seat opposite on the swivel chair, which placed him quite a lot higher than me. Instantly he was in the superior position, leaning forward, hands on his knees, demanding my full attention.

'Now then, Philippa,' he said.

I could barely breathe. He had exactly that calm, authoritative manner he used with his suspects in the interview room – firm but fair, always likeable but never to be crossed.

I thought I might fall in love with him all over again, even though I was fidgeting at the end of the bed, horribly aware of the objects behind me. Objects that might very soon be making harsh contact with my bottom.

'Can you tell me what you think I want to discuss with you this morning?'

I chewed on the inside of my cheek.

'I skipped lunch,' I muttered, fighting an absurd urge to smile. Now I understood why naughty kids caught in their mischief tended to smirk and fidget while they were being reproved. I was doing exactly the same things, and I just couldn't stop myself.

'Is something funny?'

The smile died and I shook my head.

'No, Philippa, you're right. It isn't funny at all. Your health and your well-being are serious matters. Aren't they?'

'I s'pose.'

'Look up and speak up.'

Christ, he sounded quite fierce. I swallowed and met his eye, very unwillingly.

'Yes,' I admitted.

'So why did you neglect them yesterday?'

'I told you why. I forgot. I was busy.'

'Sweetheart, we all have busy lives. You aren't unique in that. You need to organise yourself better, don't you?'

'Maybe.'

'Definitely. Look, I frequently spend my lunch hour running after stupid people who think they can outpace me. That'll make you forget to eat. But I always make sure I take a bit of time to replenish my energy levels afterwards. I never go without a meal. Because it's important. If I don't keep myself in good condition, those thieves'll be running rings around me, won't they?'

I shrugged, but my face made it pretty clear that I accepted what he said.

'Yes, they will,' he agreed with himself. 'And it's just as important for you. You have to deal with out-of-control young people. It's vital that you're on good form yourself and in control. You can't go fainting away when two of your lads decide to get into a knife fight. You're letting them down and you're letting yourself down. Aren't you?'

Dan's style was heavy on the rhetorical questioning, it seemed.

I turned down the corners of my mouth and let it droop. I hoped this was sufficient indication of penitence.

'Well?'

Obviously it wasn't.

'Yes,' I mumbled.

'So, we're going to deal with this, and let's hope it'll help you remember to schedule in time for eating in the future.'

He rolled up his sleeves to the elbow.

My knees gave way – just as well I was sitting down. The carpet was suddenly of immediate and enormous interest. Did it need vacuuming? I wanted to put my head between my knees and breathe deeply, but Dan had risen to his feet and now held out his hand to me.

I took it uncertainly and he pulled me upright and turned me to face the bed, keeping his hands on my shoulders.

'Your book recommends a warm-up before I begin properly,' he said into my ear. 'So that's what I'm going to do.'

He took my former place on the edge of the bed and brought me down over his lap. It wasn't the first time I'd been in this position, of course, but it felt so different now. Not simply exciting and sexy, but really quite humiliating. I felt small and ashamed of myself and genuinely contrite. Perhaps I would tell him and he might spare me.

'I'm really sorry,' I blurted.

His hand rubbed up and down my cotton-clad backside.

'I'm glad to hear it,' he said. 'But we have to make sure it doesn't happen again, don't we?'

'Oh,' I whined. 'It won't.'

'You need this. You told me yourself that you need it. Didn't you?'

Defeated, I sighed, 'Yes.'

'And I'm here to give you what you need, aren't I?'

'Mm hmm.'

'Now, this is just to prepare you for the real punishment. But it still isn't going to be easy to take. Think about what you've done and how you plan to improve.'

He started to spank with slow, steady strokes that made their impact without being unbearable. The loud smacking sounds were almost more embarrassing than the pain in my behind. Our elderly neighbours were obviously hard of hearing, judging by the racket their TV made, but in the still of the early morning, one never knew how far the sound might travel.

'I want you to try and keep still,' he said when I started to wriggle. 'Your book recommends that, you know? You've read it, have you?'

'A bit,' I said, sucking in a breath. He was speeding up and it made stillness very difficult to achieve.

'It says it's important to expect good behaviour when

51

you're administering punishment. It's a good idea to insist on stillness and silence. I'm not going to insist on silence yet, but it might be something to aim for in future.'

Oh, God. He was getting right into this. He envisaged it as being part of our marriage dynamic. This was what I'd hoped for … wasn't it?

I made the most of his not-enforcing-a-silence rule and began to whimper and moan as heat flushed the skin of my bottom.

'So, yes, you can make as much noise as you like, within reason. But you can stop that kicking right now.'

He smacked my bare thigh, very hard. I put my legs back down immediately.

'Do you know what else it says?' he asked me, spanking away.

'Lots of things,' I snarked.

I curled my toes and tried to keep my muscles rigid, working to deflect my brain's attention away from the increasing hurt and heat of my rear.

'It says you should stop clenching your bum cheeks. If you clench them, you get extra strokes of something much nastier than my hand. What do you think of that?'

'It's mean,' I gasped, unclenching my glutes and feeling the extra sting accordingly.

'It's effective,' he said. 'Ah, yes, this feels much better.'

He sped up and I clenched again.

'That's another stroke of the brush,' he said.

I wailed and tried to wrench my hands from his grip so I could protect my bum, but he just told me that was yet *another* stroke of the brush.

'You're like a robot without any pity,' I complained and he laughed.

'This is what you wanted, girl. This is what you've got.'

He knew I would be disappointed if he showed any sign of weakness. I supposed I ought to be grateful for his strong resolution. But gratitude wasn't finding much room to squeeze in between the harder and harder smacks.

When he stopped I let out a huge gusty sigh of relief. I was warm all over.

'There, that'll do for a warm-up,' he said, stroking and rubbing my bottom. He pulled the waistband of my shorts tight, peeking inside. 'You're a lovely shade of bright red. It suits you. Now I want you to go and stand in the corner with your hands on your head while you wait for phase two.'

'Oh, what? Why?'

My combative tone probably wasn't a good idea, but somehow the idea of hanging around facing the wall was worse than the actual spanking.

'What do you mean, why? Haven't you read that book?'

'Only the hot bits,' I admitted in a rebellious mutter.

'In other words, just the bits about spanking? So you didn't read about corner time?'

'No. What's hot about that?'

'The point is, my love, it concentrates your mind on what you have done and what is about to be done to you. It's supposed to deepen your sense of shame and penitence. And we want that, don't we?'

I didn't reply.

Since I was still bare-arsed over his lap, he gave me an encouraging smack.

'Hmm?'

'I guess so.'

'No, you don't "guess so", Philippa.'

Another smack. How did he get so hardcore so quickly?

'Yes.'

'Yes. So up you get and over to the corner.'

It felt like crossing the desert. I couldn't believe I was voluntarily placing myself in this humiliating position, but eventually there I was, nose pressed to the wall, hands on my head, back to the room.

'Good,' he said. 'Now, you're going to stay there while I have my breakfast. If you move a muscle while I'm out of the room, I will know, and I'll punish you for it. Are you going to behave?'

'Yes.'

'While you're there, I want you to think about why

54

you're being punished, and how you're going to avoid suffering the same fate for the same reason in the future. Yes?'

'Yes.'

'And you might consider adding "sir" to that.'

'God, seriously?'

'Yes, seriously.'

He left the room without enforcing it that time, but my stomach had coiled into a little spring of guilty pleasure at the idea. Sometimes, during sex, I wanted to call him 'sir', but I'd never had the nerve to say it out loud.

All my dreams were coming true in the most bizarre fashion.

So, there I was. I supposed I ought to think about the dull subject of eating at meal times. How would I ensure I didn't forget to in future? Was there an app for it? I'd look into the possibility. There. He couldn't say I wasn't taking it seriously now.

This was boring, though.

At least my bottom wasn't hurting so much. The sting began to fade straight away, but I couldn't resist peeking over my shoulder at the bed, reminding myself that it would soon be right back there.

I smelled toast and coffee and my stomach rumbled. I wanted some! Wasn't this meant to be about eating properly? But perhaps my digestion wouldn't be so good if I tucked in before bending back over. He had truly taken every detail into consideration.

It must have been about ten minutes later that he strolled back in. I was rocking to and fro on the balls of my feet, trying to enliven the silly situation I'd put myself in.

'Ready?' he said.

I nodded.

'Come to the bed, then, and lie over the pillows.'

Making me put myself into position to be spanked was a perfect piece of headspace manipulation. I felt I ought to resist, to force him to drag me to my fate, but somehow I couldn't. I knew it had to be and there was no point trying to get out of it. By hook or by crook, Dan was intent on administering my punishment.

I couldn't look at him, though, as I walked over to the bed then arched myself over the pillows with my face buried in the duvet and my bum pushed up high.

'That's it,' he said, making sure I was perfectly presented by pressing down on certain parts of my spine and shoulder blades. 'It's your job to keep your bottom right up. No trying to change positions, to make it easier on yourself. You need to work on offering it to me. I want those shorts tight and straining over your cheeks for as long as you're allowed to keep them on. Tighter. That's it.'

I pushed my arse out as far as I could, until I worried

that my thin cotton shorts might split at the seams. This had the effect of spreading my cheeks naturally apart and my gusset split my pussy lips, rubbing against my clit.

'I'm going to get you some special knickers, I think,' he said contemplatively, rubbing my bum through the material. 'A size or two smaller. Really, really tight, so they stretch very thin. Special punishment knickers, to be put on when you need a spanking.'

I tried very hard not to be incredibly turned on but I could feel my clit pulsing against the strip of cotton.

'It can all be part of the ritual,' he said.

Then, to the right of my face, I sensed that he was picking up The Belt.

'Three with this over your shorts, then three more on your bare bottom,' he decreed.

Instinctively, I clenched.

'No clenching.'

Oh, dear, this was going to be hard.

And it was – very hard. The first stroke cracked down like fire, way worse than anything he had given me before.

I moaned and swivelled my hips, taking courage in the fact that I knew the number of strokes, and it was finite and bearable.

Or was it? The second stroke made me yelp and buck forward, trying to hide my poor burning bottom from further unpleasantness.

'Up,' he said, merciless as Ming. 'Now.'

I obeyed, clinging to the duvet for dear life, and he laid the third stroke lower, so that the belt crossed my pussy lips and the bunched-up mess between them, as well as the curved lower part of my bottom. It was a really fierce stroke and I made a sobbing sound.

'OK,' said Dan. 'I know that hurt. I know it did.'

He knelt on the bed beside me and pulled down my shorts to the knees. His palm roved around my cheeks, with their three brands of fire, massaging blissfully.

'This stops you bruising,' he informed me.

'And there I was, thinking you were doing it out of the kindness of your heart,' I retorted.

He laughed and patted my sore spots gently.

'I am, in a way,' he said. 'Cruel to be kind and all that. Oh, God, I want to kiss you, but the book says not to. Not till afterwards.'

'Stupid damn book.'

'Now then. You don't want me to punish you for disrespecting the book, do you?'

I should never have ordered the bloody thing. Never.

But I pushed my body back into his loving caresses and felt myself, quite unexpectedly, ready for more of the belt.

On bare skin its tongue was twice as sharp, lashing down with instant heat. But I was ready for it, and I wanted it now. The warm-up had done a good job, loosening me up, preparing me to take harder strokes and firmer implements.

He finished the three and rubbed my bottom again, slowly and erotically. I wanted him to touch me between my legs, but it seemed that area was strictly off-limits.

'Now,' he said. 'Before I continue, let's talk. Why did you skip lunch yesterday?'

'Because I forgot. I was very busy.'

'That's understandable, but it's not the first time. In fact, it became quite an issue before. You remember?'

'Yes ... Sir.' I enjoyed saying it. Immediately the word was out, I wanted to say it again.

'So why didn't you deal with it properly then? Why didn't you find a workable solution to the problem?'

'I thought I'd be OK.'

'You thought wrong, though, didn't you?'

'I suppose so.'

His fingertips danced so sweetly along the six thick lines of heat, now starting to cool. If only he'd push them inside me ... I longed for it.

'So what are you going to do about it now? Forget again and have to be punished more severely?'

'No, Sir. I was thinking ... there might be an app for my phone. I could use the alarm feature. Have it keep going off at fifteen minute bursts after midday until I ate something.'

He patted me.

'Yes. That could work. Do that then.'

I basked in his approval.

'So,' he continued, 'now we've solved that little problem, there's just the matter of rounding off this punishment.'

He picked up the hairbrush.

I didn't really know what to expect from it. It seemed absurd to be spanked with one's own hairbrush, such an innocuous item.

'Six on your bare bottom for the original issue, plus two extra for disobedience during punishment. You're going to count them for me. Ready? Bum nice and high, please.'

I thrust it back out, full of optimism that we'd have time for a good hard screw once this was done. God knows I was dripping down there.

All my optimism vanished with the first impact of wood on flesh.

I actually screamed – it was so much more painful than I anticipated.

'Calm down, now, or there'll be more. Count it.'

He sounded rattled, maybe because he hadn't thought it would hurt me this much.

'One,' I said. 'That's very, very painful. I don't think I can do eight.'

'Can you try?'

'Oh … I don't know … oh, go on then.'

'We can take a break if you need to. But I'm going to give you all of them.'

I'm pretty sure he didn't put as much of himself into the next one. It was less shocking, but perhaps that was because I knew what to expect.

I still felt that he'd burned an oval bruise, deep into my tissues.

He rubbed me again after the third and whispered in my ear that he was proud of me.

That worked wonders. I was able to take all of the last five, in quick, hard succession, without much more than a few little whimpers before the count.

'There,' he said. 'Lesson learned?'

'Yes,' I promised. 'I'll eat my lunch every day.'

'Good girl. Now hold still for just a moment more.'

I didn't know what he had planned, but I heard a faint click and sensed a flash.

'Are you taking a photograph?'

'Yes. I thought we should keep a punishment diary. The book suggests it. It's valuable for keeping track of recurring bad behaviours and consistency of discipline. I'll post this picture and you can write up an account of it.'

'What, now?'

'Yes, now.'

'But I was hoping ...'

'Mmm, I know. But the book doesn't recommend fucking straight after punishment. It makes it seem like a reward, you see. You're going to have to wait till you get home tonight. And no touching either.'

'But that's really harsh!'

'I know. Come here, though. It doesn't say I can't give you a hug.'

I raised my groggy head and crawled over to him. I didn't want to sit down – my bottom felt very tender and hot still – so I knelt back on my heels and let him enfold me in his arms.

It was a lovely feeling, truly safe and tired and relaxed, despite the ache behind.

'Thank you,' I said, the words coming from nowhere.

'For what?' He jerked his neck back and looked down at me, quizzically amused.

'For not laughing at me about this. For taking the trouble to do it properly. For caring.'

'Hey, no worries,' he whispered, and he didn't resist me when I kissed him.

When I tried to put my hands where they weren't allowed to go, though, he broke the kiss and sat back, shaking his head and laughing.

'Stop trying to tempt me,' he said. 'You're going to have to wait. Now get to that computer and write up your account.'

I pouted. 'You aren't really going to let some stupid old book tell you what to do, are you?'

'It's a guide, love. It doesn't tell me what to do. It

makes suggestions. I choose to follow some and not others. Now, go.'

He pushed me to my feet and smacked my bottom. I winced and pulled up my shorts, retiring with what little dignity I had left to the living room and the computer desk.

I sat on a cushion to write my account, then saved it and went to get breakfast.

He left before I'd finished, giving me a rough kiss and a bit of a grab before heading out of the door.

Well, you can be sure that I didn't skip lunch. But I had more trouble with what he'd said about 'no touching'. I was OK most of the time, kept busy rehearsing a dance routine with some of the girls, but when they went home and I was left in my office finishing up reports, the remaining tenderness in my behind made me think of what Dan had done to me. And when I thought of what Dan had done to me, I also thought of what he *hadn't* done to me. And when I thought of that … well … I was alone in the building now … no appointments for an hour …

But he said no touching!

No, I was going to do this. I was going to do it properly, no cheating.

But I spent that hour squirming on my uncomfortable chair, strongly aware of the heat at my crotch and a terrible itch inside.

Dan didn't come off his shift until ten that night either. Typical.

I decided to wait for him in bed, naked. While I was there, I got hold of the dreaded book and had a flick through some of the chapters I had neglected.

Dan really had done things 'by the book'. As well as corner time, it laid out a range of non-spanking (and therefore unsexy) options to add to the punishment. None of them sounded very appealing. A note in the back advertised a further manual of 'Advanced Techniques' with some scary-looking chapter headings. Enhanced Corner Time. Using the Cane. Sexual Discipline. What the hell could sexual discipline be?

I was pondering this when I heard keys in the front door.

I tossed the book back on to his bedside table and tried to arrange myself into as alluring a pose as I could.

I heard him call my name.

'In here.'

He was smiling broadly when he appeared in the doorway.

'Ah, I see.'

He came in and started to undress.

'Thank God for that,' he said. 'I thought for a moment I'd gone too far this morning and you'd walked out on me. I had nightmares about you citing what we did in the divorce petition.'

'That would hardly be fair,' I said, enjoying the strip-tease. 'Since it was my idea.'

'I know. But it's so unusual in this day and age. People would be shocked.'

'Yeah. Probably more than if it was me spanking you. They'd probably think that was fine.'

'But I wouldn't.'

'It doesn't appeal to you then?'

'No. Because I haven't got a cute, round arse that turns bright red really quickly.'

He was undressed now and he reached out for me, so that I giggled and hid under the covers.

'Lie on your front,' he said, coming in after me. 'I want to make sure I didn't bruise you.'

I rolled over and let him inspect the state of my rear. He rubbed and patted and prised the cheeks apart to check inside them.

'No visible damage,' he said. 'You'd never know it happened. Maybe it's slightly pinker than usual. Were you uncomfortable today? Sore?'

'No, not really sore. I was just a bit more *aware* of it than usual, if you know what I mean.'

'I thought people were meant to not be able to sit down for a week after a good hiding. What the hell would you have to do to achieve that, I wonder?'

'I don't think I want to know.'

'No. I don't suppose you do. So, what did you have for lunch?'

'Falafel from the van across the road. Orange juice. Pear.'

'That'll do nicely.' He pushed my thighs further apart and crouched down, examining the scene. 'Oh, look. Nice and wet.'

He kissed me between the lips and stuck his tongue deep inside me. I moaned and raised myself slightly, begging for more.

'Have you been hot for this all day?' he asked, pulling me up on to all fours.

I nodded and wiggled my hips.

'So have I,' he said, gliding into my well-lubricated passage without a moment's hesitation. 'Get ready, love. I'm going to give you what you've been waiting for.'

27 July

I woke up all stiff and sore between the legs, with a big smile on my face.

What a night.

But what a day I was going to have. I'd say, Thank God it's Friday, but I work Saturdays too, and Dan often works Sundays, so that five days on, two days off thing isn't really us.

He was already at work, so I started my day with only the memory of a long, hot night spent mainly on my knees, with occasional moves on to my back. It seemed that what we did yesterday morning had really started a fire in Dan. He couldn't get enough of me.

I made it through the working day without falling asleep somehow.

When I got home, he was there, and dinner was in the oven, judging by the savour of the air around me.

'Oh, smells lovely,' I said, coming in and putting my bags down on the kitchen table.

'Yeah, I thought we could have something special tonight. All your favourites. There's an open bottle in the fridge, if you want to pour yourself a glass.'

I have to say, whatever this domestic discipline thing was doing for me, it was also turning him into the ideal husband. There were fresh flowers on the living-room mantelpiece too.

I sat down on the bench with a large glass of Pinot Grigio and watched him flit around with his apron on until he was satisfied that everything was under control.

Then he pulled a notebook and pen from the drawer and sat down opposite me.

'What's that for?' I asked, a little confused. 'You going to interview me?'

He smiled. 'I've had enough of that for one day, to be honest. Massive haul of stolen goods, six guys in for questioning ... anyway, never mind that. This is about us.'

'You want to make a list?'

'Yeah, I suppose I do. You brought this whole discipline thing up because you said there were things you wanted to change about yourself. Well, not yourself, but, you know, you wanted to modify your behaviour in certain ways.'

'Yes.'

'So, tell me what those ways are. I'm thinking we need a sensible list that we can refer to, otherwise I might accidentally punish you for something you don't think is fair, or I might let something slip that you really want help with. Make sense?'

'Yes. God. What is with you? You're like the man with the plan. I never thought it'd take you this way.'

He put down the pen, looking mildly injured.

'I'm doing this for you.'

'I know. OK. Well, the main thing was my temper. I get irritable and snap and lash out at you for things that aren't your fault. I want to stop doing that. But counting to ten and all that doesn't work. So that's number one.'

'Right.' He started scribbling in his book. 'I'm going to add the one about not eating. And not taking care of yourself in general. Getting enough sleep, not working two hours past hometime, that kind of thing.'

'You know how it is,' I protested.

'No. My shift ends and I head for the locker room. No exceptions. It's a good working rule and worth keeping.'

'But I don't have a new shift coming to relieve me.'

'No, but you're not superhuman and you need to know when to stop.'

I huffed a bit, but he had a point. I'd worn myself down to a tearful nub last Christmas and spent the holidays in bed with an exhaustion-aggravated bout of flu.

'Go on then,' I sighed.

'Anything else you want to add?' he asked.

'I can't think of anything specific. Can we add to the list as we go along? As things occur to us?'

'Of course.' He shut the notebook. 'Now, would you lay the table for me, love? And after that, I'm going to type all this up. I'm going to make a proper contract type of thing. A list of rules.'

'Rules for me?'

'Yes. Rules for you.'

'How formal,' I said with a light shudder.

'I want to do this right.'

'I know you do,' I said. 'I should have known you would.'

1 *August*

I've followed the rules pretty well over the last few days. Summer holidays are coming up, which has kept my mood upbeat and my temper sweet.

A couple of times I've almost fallen off the wagon – a few minutes late here and there, nothing more – but Dan has just uttered a word of warning and I've jumped into line.

It's exciting. I like the feeling of being on a tightrope, trying to keep my eyes ahead and my head level. I mustn't fall!

But of course nobody can walk a tightrope forever, and my balance is getting very, very wobbly.

I got home yesterday and found one of those 'While You Were Out' delivery notes on the doormat. Always annoying, at the best of times, and I'd had a hard day so I swore at it as I read the instruction to come and collect it from the post office.

'What's wrong?'

Dan was right behind me, frowning over my shoulder.

'Oh. That's for me. Can you pick it up tomorrow?'

I tutted.

'I suppose so,' I said ungraciously. 'It'll mean going into town after work though.'

'Never mind, eh?' said Dan, in a tone that I was starting to recognise as dangerous. 'If you'd rather, I'll get them to throw it through the area car window while I'm out chasing down a twocker. Would that be easier for you?'

I didn't say anything but flung the card at the hall table, not bothering to retrieve it when it missed and fluttered down to the floor.

'I'm considering issuing a warning,' said Dan. 'You need to calm down. It's a minor inconvenience, not an outrage.'

What was a bloody outrage was the way he thought he had the right to lecture me.

Oh. But I'd given him that right, hadn't I? I wanted him to work with me on minimising precisely this kind of overreaction. But in the heat of my irritation I couldn't find that headspace and instead I sulked and flounced around the kitchen, banging pots and pans when I emptied the dishwasher.

This seemed to do the trick and, by the time he came in to help me prepare dinner, I was all smiles and 'how was your day?' again.

So I got away with that one.

Or so I thought.

Today was hot – the hottest day of the summer so far – and lunch at the lido was looking very, very good. I grabbed a sunbed, slapped on the lotion and settled down, waiting for the café waiter to come out with my order of a crab salad and a glass of sparkling orange juice. This was the bloody life, no two ways about it. Splashing from the pool, warmth on my skin, pure chill-out away from the city stress …

Oh, shit. I sat upright. I was supposed to go and pick up Dan's parcel.

Ugh. I was supposed to pound the burning concrete all the way up to the sorting office, sweating like fury, and then lug the thing – which could be any inconvenient size or shape – back. And eat lunch. All in one hour.

It was too much to ask. He'd have to wait. Why couldn't he have it redelivered, some time when his shift pattern allowed? He was unreasonable. It was not my job to run around after him. Etcetera. Ah, here was my crab salad. Yum.

Well, maybe I could pick it up after work. Except the office, I dimly recalled, closed at four. There definitely wasn't time now. I had to get back a bit early to set up the mock job interviews I was running.

I tried to forget about it, tell myself it would be OK, I could do it tomorrow, but the crab salad didn't go down quite as well as I'd hoped because I was suddenly very nervous, in a gastric kind of way.

Deep down, I knew that I hadn't 'forgotten' to pick it up. I'd deliberately chosen to go to the lido instead. The question was, should I tell Dan that? Or should I pretend it had completely slipped my mind?

This dilemma kept demanding that I wrestle with it between mock interviews, all afternoon. It was tough pretending to be the boss when I suspected I might be spending the evening with my knickers around my ankles and my bottom on fire.

I made my final decision in the ladies' toilets at the end of the session. I wanted Dan to know the extent of my defiance. I wanted him to punish me.

I was going to tell him.

I was almost too anxious and excited to keep still on the bus home. It was so hot that I could imagine the window frames and fittings melting around us and I shifted my damp thighs uncomfortably on the fuzzy upholstery, wondering how much more uncomfortable they might feel tomorrow morning. This thought was disturbingly arousing and I hoped my fellow passengers, wedged up against me on both sides, couldn't smell anything untoward.

I found myself wondering if anyone else on this bus was in for a spanking tonight. What about the bored-looking young woman in the office suit, texting away? Was she trying to plead with her partner to be lenient with her? Or the middle-aged hipster with the sideburns and the sweary T-shirt – was somebody going to put him over their knee for being provocative in public? Or perhaps they were doing the spanking. The woman with the half-dozen shopping bags at her feet looked as if she might wield a mean strap.

By the time we reached my stop, I'd involved practically everyone on the bus in my secret world of fetish. I felt a bit guilty about it, to be honest, but it was so much on my mind I couldn't think of anything else.

Dan wouldn't be home till eight, so I made sure I had his favourite meal on the go and a glass of wine poured, soft music pouring from the speakers, and so on. Not that he really likes soft music. So that was probably not the best idea. The visible stockings, promising interesting underwear at the top of the suspenders, were sure to stand me in good stead, though. Distraction was always a good technique.

He might even have forgotten about the parcel.

But no, if he had, I was still going to bring it up. Otherwise I would feel that I had wasted all this effort, somehow.

'Hey, hey, hey, what's all this?' he wondered, walking into the living room and sniffing the air. 'Mexican steak?'

'Your favourite,' I purred, standing in the kitchen doorway in the most siren-like pose I could muster.

I wanted to laugh at the instant suspicion that clouded his eyes.

'Have I forgotten something? An anniversary or birthday?'

'No. I just felt in the mood for something special.'

He was right in front of me by then and he grabbed my arse and pulled me into a long, sultry snog, the kind that usually ends up on the sofa with clothes strewn all over the floor.

Much as my body and mind chorused, 'Yes! Hot sex! Result!' I could still perceive the nagging voice of my conscience behind it all.

But sex first, yeah? Why not?

Because the steak was burning – that was why not!

'Ohhh,' I wailed, running back into the kitchen, where flames had started leaping around the edge of the pan. I doused it with a damp cloth, but the steaks weren't exactly as rare as Dan usually liked them.

Never mind. He made a valiant effort with his knife and fork and we laughed it all off. 'How-was-your-day?' took us through the meal to ice-cream, and that was where the road started to get rocky. (It was Rocky Road ice-cream too – appropriate.)

'Oh, did you pick up that package?' he asked.

He posed it as an afterthought but, in retrospect, I

think he'd been building up to it, lulling me into a false sense of security before pouncing. There was a certain brightness to his eyes despite the casual tone.

'Oh! Oh, God, no, sorry. I –' I was so close to saying 'forgot''– didn't.'

He didn't say anything, damn him. I needed him to throw me a lifeline, ask me if I had forgotten, say it didn't matter and I could do it tomorrow.

'I'll do it tomorrow,' I offered.

'Yes.' That was it. No more.

He dug his spoon into the ice-cream and left it there.

'It was such a beautiful day,' I said, half in defence, half as a change of subject.

'Too beautiful for keeping promises.'

Oh, if he was just going to *sulk* instead of ... the other thing ...

'It's no big deal,' I snapped. 'I don't suppose another day will make a difference.'

'No, Pip, don't take that tone with me. I'm not in the wrong here.'

'In the wrong? It's a stupid fucking parcel, that's all. What's in it? Explosives?'

'Philippa.' A low growl.

But somehow I couldn't stop talking myself into trouble.

I stood up, eyeing the door to the hallway nervously, my fight-or-flight response signalling 'flight'.

'If it's so important to you, why don't you get it rede-livered? You've got the day off on Friday. You can reschedule it online. That would have been the obvious thing to do anyway, but it wouldn't occur to you, I suppose, when you've got Muggins here to run around after you.' I started walking away.

'Where do you think you're going?'

He sounded calm, but absolutely authoritative.

I halted in my tracks.

'Nowhere.'

'That's right. You're going nowhere.'

'What? For God's sake, forget it, Dan. You're ruining what could be a lovely evening.' I'd lost it by now, shouting and gesticulating like Basil Fawlty. I disliked myself for it, but how could I make myself stop?

'*I'm* ruining it?'

'You're overreacting!' I bawled.

He laughed at that, then pointed to the sofa in our open-plan lounge-diner.

'All right, Philippa, overreact to this,' he said, not raising his voice a decibel. 'Go and bend over the arm.'

'I ...'

'Now.'

Here I was, at a crossroads that felt enormously significant.

I could say no. He had no recourse, after all. I knew he wouldn't force me. It would take just a few calm, reasonable words. Or, if I carried on shouting and screaming, he would probably just walk away, go to the pub, like he always used to.

But I didn't want that. I hated those hours he spent at the pub while I paced the flat, full of rage, then full of remorse, then full of facepalm.

I hated having to apologise and have him wonder aloud what got into me.

Of course, I loved the make-up sex.

But perhaps we could have that too, without all the icky in-between stuff?

I looked at his face. It was resolute and stern. It was everything I had fantasised.

I went to the sofa.

I looked over my shoulder at him. He was watching me.

It was a giddy feeling. If I voluntarily put myself over the arm, I was making a profound statement. *I put myself in your hands. I accept your authority.*

It was too hard. And I felt ridiculous, like a character in one of the hokey spanking stories I was always browsing online. And I felt *guilty*, as if I was dancing on the Pankhurst graves in hobnailed boots.

But, look, I had asked for this.

'Philippa.'

His voice acted like a hand between my shoulder blades.

I bent, feeling the swishy hem of my dress rise up my bared thigh.

I listened to him walk up to me.

'It's not that you've done something terrible, Philippa,' he said.

I flinched when he put a hand on my thigh, just where it met the dress, and stroked through the material.

'Of course it's not that. That's trivial. It's the way you behaved when I asked you. Defensive, straight away. Trying to blame me. Getting yourself wound up. This is what you want to change, isn't it?'

I nodded, too embarrassed by my position to speak.

'It's like the divisional Christmas lunch. Remember that? You were too hungover to go. But that was *my* fault, apparently, because I should have somehow stopped you from drinking too much with your girlfriends the night before. I should have picked you up earlier. I should have called you to make sure you weren't too legless. I should have done this, I should have done that. No, Philippa. I'm not having any more of it. You are going to take responsibility for your own behaviour, and if I have to make you, then so be it. It's what you want, isn't it?'

I nodded again, stung by his horribly accurate and relevant memory.

Not as stung as I was a moment later, when he lifted my dress to my waist and began to smack my bottom over my prettiest, laciest knickers.

He didn't even comment on them, let alone allow them to distract him.

Instead, he spanked away until they felt tight and uncomfortable and prickly.

Once I started ouching and twitching under his hand, he stopped and pulled them down.

'Stay right there,' he said firmly. 'Don't move a muscle.'

I heard him walk through to the kitchen and scrabble in the drawers. How strange. What could he have in mind?

When he came back, he laid something flat and cool and made, I supposed, of wood against my warmed cheeks.

'This might be painful,' he warned me. 'But you're getting ten good hard ones. No excuses.'

He was right about the pain. There was some kind of fundamental antagonism between skin and wood. I kicked and gasped and earned two extras, but I managed to hold myself down for the full complement, working through the deep-seated soreness and heat, taking my medicine.

He lectured me throughout and, while I couldn't have said I was listening very closely at the time, when I thought about it afterwards, I recalled every single word. It seemed that words plus spanks gave a much more lasting effect than words alone. This was a shaming realisation, but one I had to accept if I was going to make a success of the project.

Once he'd put down the wooden thing – a spatula, I

noticed – I expected him to send me to the stupid corner, or the computer to write the stupid journal entry, but he didn't. Instead, he let his hand linger on my bottom, stroking it, then one of his fingers drifted in between the cheeks, making me shiver.

I heard his breathing quicken. His hand slid down inside my thighs. I could almost feel his indecision, almost feel the unruly twitch of his pulse.

Finally, he said, 'Ah, fuck it,' in a rough-edged voice and I heard his trousers fall, with a clink of belt buckle, down to his ankles.

I felt a charge of victorious lust right between my legs. He had beaten me and now I had beaten him. His grip on my hips made me snarl with triumph and when he pushed into me, quickly and without finesse, I hissed.

Whoever wrote that book had better self-control than Dan.

Whoever wrote that book was able to look at his woman's rosy-red upturned arse without the blood rushing to a certain part of his patriarchal anatomy. Or so he said. Personally, I think he was lying.

Dan definitely didn't share his imperviousness. He thrust away, hard and fast, grunting with the effort of it. His pelvis slapped up against my too-warm cheeks, heating them even more, and he put a hand on the scruff of my neck and held me down until he heard the muffled, garbled beginnings of my orgasm.

That was all he needed to start pumping even faster, until he collapsed with all his weight on top of me so that the sofa arm pressed uncomfortably into my stomach.

'Oh, God,' he panted, his damp cheek sticking to mine. 'Oh, God, Pip. I don't think I'm up to this.'

'Hey,' I wheezed, barely able to get the breath out of my severely compressed lungs.

He took the hint, heaved himself off me and landed with a thud on the sofa. He grabbed my hands and drew me on to his lap – not over it, this time. The deep-seated tenderness from the spatula-spanking made me gasp a little, but I liked the feel of it, right inside me, a living *aide-mémoire*.

He wrapped his arms tightly around me and buried his face in my shoulder for a few moments. When he withdrew it, he looked sheepish.

'I'm sorry,' he said.

'It really hurt,' I said, 'but that was what I needed. Don't be sorry.'

'No, not that,' he said with a little snuffle of a laugh. 'I'd have given you twice as many strokes if you'd given me a hint of defiance. No, I mean … afterwards.'

'Oh, you shouldn't be sorry about that. I'm certainly not.'

His lips twisted in a quick smile but his eyes were troubled.

'I feel like I've fucked up. No, don't make some silly

joke, I'm serious. You want this and I want to help you. If I turn it into a kinky sex game because I can't control my, uh, urges, then ...'

'Oh, don't be so hard on yourself, love.'

'Well, that's it. It's *you* I'm supposed to be hard on.'

'But it gives you a hard-on.'

'Oh, shut *up*, Pip.'

I buttoned my lip. He sounded on the verge of tears, bless him.

'I mean, if I'm going to do this, I want to do it right.'

That's very Dan, that is. He's not a man to do anything by halves, and he doesn't shirk the difficult bits.

'Yes, but that book ... it's only one way of doing things. One guy's way. We don't have to follow it to the letter, do we? We can tailor our own version.'

'Yeah, I know, I agree. But it's too soon for that. I'm feeling my way ... yes, yes, I know, literally. Don't say it. I need the book, just while I'm establishing my own rules and routines.'

'It's like a hand to hold?'

'Yeah.'

'While the other hand is busy ... elsewhere.'

'Pip, you seem remarkably cheerful for somebody who's just been soundly punished. Why is that?'

I nuzzled his neck and kissed him. I felt madly, blissfully, hormonally in love with him. I mean, more than usually. It was weird.

'Because it makes me feel loved. How upside-down is that? I can't really explain it any better. And I don't mean I didn't already feel loved – because I did. But it makes me feel really deep-down cared for.'

He blinked at me a few times in rapid succession.

'Right,' he said. 'That's funny. It's something the book mentioned, but it also said I had to be careful afterwards, to make sure you realised I didn't dislike you or, or, you know, wasn't doing it to ... Well, the thing is, I'm supposed to cheer *you* up afterwards. I'm supposed to tell you everything's OK and I love you and everything's forgotten and forgiven. But ... it's like ... you're doing that. I'm confused.'

'It's early days, darling. It's a learning curve, for both of us.'

I had to smother the desire to make some pathetic joke about how he was learning about my curves. Perhaps I should add that to the sin list. Inappropriate punning will be punished. God, I really can't help myself.

'I'm sorry, love. I don't mean to be a dithering plank. I want to be all manly and firm-chinned and resolute and all that. I feel I'm failing in that.'

'You're the manliest, most resolute and firmest-chinned man on the planet, Daniel Wheatley. Don't let anyone tell you different.'

He seemed happy with that.

3 August

I was optimistic about the direction all this was taking. And then I took a look at Book 2 of The Book.

I wasn't supposed to look at it.

Dan has been guarding it with his life since I brought it back from the sorting office. He wrestled it off me within seconds and disappeared into the bedroom with it.

When I followed him, he clutched it to his chest and ordered me out.

'Can't I see? It's my business, surely.'

'No, it isn't. I need to inwardly digest it before I can share it. Pip, don't. If you come any closer, I'll have to, to spank you.'

He sounded too anxious to be convincing, but I

thought I'd let him have his way in this precisely because of that. Poor Dan. I wanted to make this easier for him.

But would making it easier for him make it harder for me?

I had to know.

So, having two hours before he was expected home from his shift, I went on a book hunt.

The obvious place to look was the bedroom, but Dan was a police officer with ambitions to be a detective, so I supposed he'd eschew the obvious. Or maybe a double bluff? I started in the bedroom.

I looked in his sock drawer, wardrobe, under the bed, in the box where he keeps the sex toys ... nada.

I had a similar lack of success in the cutlery drawer, the bathroom cabinet, behind the PlayStation, inside the tumble dryer. This book had vanished.

Had he taken it to work with him? Surely not. Imagine the furore, should he be caught with it in the locker room.

I had to try and think outside the box. Where would I never look in a million years?

It took a while for inspiration to strike, but when it did it was harder and more exquisite than any of Dan's belt licks.

The box file in which I kept all details of my tax affairs and investments.

I took it off the top bookshelf and laughed with fiendish

delight to find it several times heavier than I expected. When I opened the spring clip, there it lay. *Advanced Discipline Techniques: A Handbook for Marital Harmony*.

The cover was very plain and it was spiral-bound like someone's dissertation – but it was obviously cheaply self-published, by necessity, so this wasn't too surprising.

I skimmed over the annoying foreword with its continuing antediluvian insistence on fixed gender roles and patriarchal rule and went straight to chapter one. Caning. Eek.

Chapter two, then.

But I couldn't focus on chapter two, which was a bit dull and about chore lists and micro-management. Something kept tugging me back to chapter one.

The cane, that instrument of legend and lore. Its reputation was enough to make strong men quake. Before my time, it had been the ultimate sanction in school – well, the penultimate, I suppose, expulsion being more serious – something to contain the uncontainable elements of youth.

I couldn't imagine being called upon to use it on a young person now. I certainly couldn't work with children if I was expected to do so. But how did I feel about it being used on me?

I'd seen it in films and historical dramas on TV and the ferocious swish and crack were noises that both terrified and excited me. I'd often felt myself blushing and having to look away. The idea of it exerted a power and fascination over me that I found both repulsive and compelling.

When I pictured Dan, in his uniform, maybe, or his best suit, wielding the slim, crook-handled monster, I had to put my fist in my mouth to suppress a moan.

But he would never use one of those things on me. It would *hurt*.

God, yes, it would hurt, and the pain would last. Imagine the stripes and the soreness and the difficulty sitting down for days afterwards ... imagine how chastened I would feel every time my bottom met some surface or other. And I didn't have to imagine how wet it was making me.

Damn.

Did I actually want to be caned?

I decided I'd better flick swiftly on. Flick the pages of the book, I mean, in case you think I'm referring to something else.

I ignored the boring chore chapter, but the next chapter was even worse. Toilet training. Was this serious?

Before I knew what I was doing, I'd picked up my thick laundry-marker pen and scored through the whole chapter.

The nib hovered over chapter four as well. 'Anal Discipline', what the fuck? But I read the first paragraph and put the pen down, my hands suddenly shaky.

This was the most depraved, the most horrible, the most humiliating thing I'd ever read about. But it was turning me on. Oh, God. What kind of person was I?

Butt plugs. Lubricants with sting-factor. Ginger root! *Ginger root?* The idea of putting any of these things up my bottom made me squirm in my chair. But the squirming was accompanied by a heat and an undeniable juiciness. I tensed my sphincter muscles for all I was worth, but that only aroused me all the more.

I stood up, opened the window, tried to get a breath of air, but the day had been still and humid and, even now the sun was setting, it hadn't cooled a great deal. I held on the window frame and visualised myself in the corner with a plug of root ginger up my arse. How on earth would that feel? I couldn't really imagine it, but I *could* imagine Dan looking on with his arms folded and a smirk of satisfaction on his face as he watched me writhe and, oh, God, it was too much.

I ran to the bedroom and got the toy box out from the bottom drawer.

Before a minute had elapsed, I was doubled over on the carpet – couldn't even take the time to get comfortable on the bed – running a vibrator around my clit then thrusting it inside me. But what would it feel like, I wondered as I pushed and pulled, what would it feel like in that other opening? I yanked it out and reached between my thighs, trying to line the tip up with the tight pucker inside my cheeks. It was difficult to do – one really needed a partner for this, if unpractised in the art – and I lost courage before I'd gone much beyond a tentative nudge.

I reverted to my normal techniques and came, tearfully and breathlessly, on the carpet, my cheek pressed into the scratchy pile.

I felt groggy for a long time, overheated and sticky in my clothes. Eventually I dragged myself into the shower and began to think about covering my tracks.

If Dan came home to find the book out on the coffee table …

Not that I was going to be able to keep my secret perusal under wraps for long. After all, I'd crossed out a whole chapter. Presumably he would notice. Or perhaps he hadn't read that far and he would think the author had done it … Hmm. But I mustn't lie or look for ways to wriggle out of trouble. That wasn't what all this was about.

I'd defaced his book and I'd have to own up to it.

And he couldn't do anything advanced yet, surely. No running before we could walk.

All the same, I took care to replace it in the box file and stack it carefully on the shelf, only making it into the kitchen to think about supper when I heard his key in the lock.

It was both of our customs, when we were the last

one home, to try and establish what might be cooking by sniffing the air.

Dan was no different, peering around the kitchen wall to try and work out what he would be eating later.

'Running late,' I said apologetically, a saucepan in each hand.

I put up my face to be kissed.

'Busy day?' he asked, stepping back once the greeting was performed.

'Well, not busy, as such, but … distracting. Spaghetti carbonara? OK?'

'Sure.' He flicked his eyes, quickly but unmistakably, towards the top of the bookshelf. 'So, what was so distracting?' He put his arms around my waist and whispered into my ear. 'Not got a secret lover, have you? You don't usually shower in the evening.' He took a big lungful of the citrus-scented shampoo in my hair.

'I do if I've been outside with the crew all afternoon, doing basketball hoops.'

It was only half a lie. I had, in fact, been doing that.

'Right.' He chuckled and turned away. 'Yeah, carbonara. Got any garlic bread?'

He wandered out into the living room area and flicked on the TV.

I wondered when he would find the book with the scribbled-out chapter.

Tonight?

Tomorrow?

Next week?

I put the pasta on to boil, threw the bacon into the pan.

I had to bring the subject up, or I would be pussy-footing around it all night.

'So, how's it going with the new book? Any important insights?' I poked my head around the kitchen units, mock-casual.

As I did so, he dropped on to the sofa a long, thin paper package he'd been holding.

'What's that?'

He coughed. 'Just, um, nothing. Why are you asking me about the book? Guilty conscience?'

I left the cooking to itself and headed to the sofa, wanting a closer look at the mystery shopping.

'Oh, y'know, curious,' I mumbled, peering over the sofa back. The bag was plain brown paper, the top sello-taped over. Whatever was inside was long and very thin. 'Did you go shopping after work?'

'The bacon'll burn,' he said.

'Go and see to it then.' I lunged for the package and he snatched it up, clutching it to his chest. 'If you're so worried.'

'It's not for prying eyes,' he said, shaking his head at me maddeningly.

'Now I definitely have to see it,' I said.

I ran around the sofa, but he had it behind his back

93

and was crossing the room too swiftly for me. He was going to get away from me and I wouldn't know if it was … what I thought it was …

I leapt and made a desperate grab. It tore the paper and, even though I ended up falling over myself on to the floor, I had achieved my objective.

I could see exactly what the brown paper covered. It was a lighter brown, sleek and slender, varnished and vicious. It was a cane.

'Happy now?' said Dan, ripping off the rest of the bag and swishing his purchase through the air.

I was dumbfounded, a pile of sexually charged fear on the wood laminate.

'Is that … for me?' I whispered, once I'd sorted out which limb belonged where.

He put the tip of it beneath my chin and tapped, very gently, but I nearly wet myself.

'Who else?' he said. His smile was teasing, with an underlying chill factor that made me shiver.

'You have to know how to use one of those things,' I said. 'The book says so. You have to practise. You can't just start using them willy-nilly.'

Oh, God. I have no talent for crime. Massive talent for self-incrimination though.

'And how,' he said, removing the cane from beneath my chin and tracing the outline of my neck and shoulders with its tip, 'would you know what the book says?'

I swallowed. 'I found it,' I said. 'I had a look at it.'

He put the cane down on the table.

'You found it? How? I hid it so well.'

'Not well enough, detective. Shit, the bacon's burning. Give me five.'

'I'll give you more than five, you little sneak.'

He followed me into the kitchen, saying nothing while I turned off the heat and tipped the bacon out of the pan for it to cool.

'Pass us the eggs,' I said warily.

'Here. Cream?'

'Please.'

I could tell how tense my shoulders were because beating up the carbonara sauce became quite painful quite soon.

'You must have known I'd look for it,' I said, putting down the fork and trying to stretch my cramping muscles.

'Well, duh,' he said. He came up behind me and massaged my shoulder blades, ah, blissful. 'That's why I put it in that box. Psychology.'

'You should have used reverse psychology. Put it somewhere dead obvious.'

'I thought of that, but then I had to reverse the reverse psychology. I'm not sure how many degrees I went through before I chose my final hiding place. At least seven hundred and twenty. Maybe more.'

'Is it so bad that I found it? It does affect me, after all.'

His fingertips sank deep into my tissues, freeing me from my locked-tightness.

'No,' he said contemplatively. 'I guess. I just wanted to surprise you with a few things.'

I tensed again, ouching as his fingers dug into me.

'Like that awful toilet stuff? I bloody well hope not! That is no-go, ever, in a million years, so don't even –'

He silenced my increasingly hysterical ranting with a light smack to my behind.

'Oi,' he said. 'Calm down. Nobody's doing anything you don't agree to. I thought we'd established that?'

'Yeah, and then you go and buy a cane.'

He nuzzled up closer, resting his chin on my shoulder, clasping his hands around my stomach.

'I suppose I might have given in to hope on that one,' he said.

'Hope?'

'I like the thought of seeing your bum all striped. It's a bit of a fantasy of mine.'

I nearly cricked my neck turning to look at his face.

'You have these fantasies too? You're not just doing it to, you know, humour me?'

'No, not at all. I'm getting quite into it now. At first I was so worried that you would change your mind and start thinking of me as some kind of monster. It kind of put me off. But you seem pretty OK with things as they've gone, so ...'

'I am. I am OK with them. And if you enjoy it, I'm even more OK with it.'

'That's all right then. Are you going to make this dinner or do I have to take over?'

I wrenched my attention back to the kitchen counter while Dan loped off in the direction of the living room. He came back just as I was mixing the sauce ingredients.

'By the way,' he said, 'what's your vibrator doing in the bathroom sink?'

My face flamed. I'd forgotten to put it away after washing it.

'Oh, uh, just lying there, I expect,' I said.

He came up close again, speaking low and slow into my ear.

'Seeing to yourself, were you, after reading all about the cane? Well, I've got a new rule, Pip. No more secret self-pleasuring. You have to wait until I get home.'

'But that's not fair,' I blurted to his retreating back.

'Fair?' He turned and grinned. 'Is it fair that you get to make all the rules? I don't think so. God, I'm starving. Is that thing ready yet?'

5 August

I got away lightly the night I discovered Book 2. He didn't punish me for it, because he accepted that there was no rule about playing hide and seek, although it had disappointed him that he wouldn't be able to 'surprise' me with something hideous like stinging nettles in my knickers. Warped sense of humour that man of mine has.

Mind you, it's no worse than mine.

I say there was no punishment, but in a funny way there was.

Obviously, the Affair of the Vibrator had affected him in some way, and he spent the evening, after we went to bed, taking me to the brink of orgasm and then pulling back. He did this three times, until I was a red-faced, teary-eyed mess of frustration, then he kissed me all over and said it served me right.

I kicked him in the shin and then he let me come at last. Romance isn't dead, you know.

The next day, he was on night shift, so I didn't see much of him. Instead, I did more surreptitious reading of Book 2, and more fantasising about the final chapter.

I wanted to know about this ginger thing, and yet I also really didn't want to know. I went as far as going to the kitchen and peeling a ginger finger, but then I got scared and threw it in the sink. I really wanted Dan to come home – I was ragingly horny and forbidden from relieving myself. In fact, I'd been ragingly horny ever since we started with this domestic discipline thing. The link seemed clear.

The more I thought about being bent over and caned with my bum stuffed full of root vegetable matter, the more desperate I was to welcome my husband home.

And yet, I really dreaded his doing any of these things. It was too paradoxical to think about.

I was asleep before he came home, but we both had today off.

We had an excursion planned – a trip to the seaside, involving calling on old friends from university days. I'd been looking forward to it for weeks.

'Are you going to bring your cane?' I asked teasingly as he looked around the room for his iPod and charger.

'Not a bad idea,' he said.

I'd been joking, but he actually went downstairs, holding it in his hand for all to see, and put it in the back seat of the car.

'I can't believe you did that,' I gasped, staring at him on his return.

'Your idea,' he said casually. 'And I know what you're like on car journeys. Thought it might come in handy.'

'OK, I'll drive,' I said, although I loathed driving and avoided it at all costs.

'No need for that,' he said, swooping on the iPod when he saw it on the kitchen shelf. 'It's only an hour down the motorway. I'm happy to take the wheel.'

Take the wheel. Something about the way he said it sounded both sinister and exciting. I could tell he had some kind of agenda in mind, and the cane might well be part of it.

'Have you programmed the SatNav?'

Most of our vehicle-bound fallings-out involved directions wrongly or hastily given. The SatNav had saved our marriage on more than one occasion.

'We won't need it,' he said briskly. 'It's motorway all the way, then downhill to the beach. Easy as pie.'

'Have you ever made a pie?' I grumbled. 'They're actually quite complicated.'

He laughed, then clapped his hands.

'Got the towels? Picnic basket? Sunblock? Come on. The sun'll go in.'

I eyed the cane on the back seat as Dan hit the motorway slip road, singing along to a rock track I didn't much like. I supposed it was there to warn me. He wouldn't actually use the thing. All the same, it added ice to my veins, seeing it lying there like a lithe brown snake.

Better a brown snake than Whitesnake, though, I thought crossly, wishing Dan would turn off the CD player.

Once we were in the middle lane of the road, he began really belting the song out and I found myself both irritated and fearful. Because my own driving is so bad, it always makes me anxious to think that Dan might not be giving the road his full attention.

'Watch out!' I kept shouting, every time a car in another lane indicated in front of us, no matter how far ahead they were.

'I have eyes,' he said. 'I can see.'

He went back to singing.

I snapped off the CD player.

'Hey, what's up? I was listening to that.'

'It's horrible.'

'Then all you have to do is say, "Darling husband, I'm not enjoying this music – shall we change it to something we both like?" *Et voilà*. Problem solved.'

101

'You were yelling your head off. You wouldn't have heard me.'

'*Yelling*? I was singing, Pip. Singing.'

'You'd never have changed the CD.'

'You'd never have asked. You just go straight for the off button. No "I don't like this", no "what about a different CD?" Just nought to pissed off, with nothing in between. It's ... look.'

He hit the indicator, to my surprise, and then I saw that we were leaving the motorway and heading towards a roadside service area.

'We don't need petrol,' I said with alarm, suddenly awfully conscious of that cane in the back seat.

'I'm not getting petrol.' He parked at the edge of the services, near a pine wood, and turned to me. 'Isn't this what we're trying to change?' he said. 'Bad temper, flying off the handle, overreacting?'

'All I did was turn off the CD player.' But I knew he had a valid point. I could have mentioned that I didn't like the music. He wasn't so unreasonable that he would have carried on listening to it. Why hadn't I done that?

He smiled at me and tickled my cheek. I tried to duck away, tried to hide my shame and dread and ... my God, I must be blushing fit to light up the dark forest behind us.

'All you did was turn off the CD player *with attitude*,' he said. 'If I let this pass, you won't thank me for it. You'll think you've got one over on me and congratulate yourself and push things further and further until we fall out seriously. Do you want me to let that happen?'

I swallowed. I didn't. Actually, I really didn't. But I couldn't tell him that – my pride stood in the way.

'It's so trivial,' I muttered.

'Come on, Philippa, be fair. This is exactly what you wanted. You can't pick it up and put it down when it suits you. I wouldn't be doing this properly if I let it go. And you know I want to do this properly. Don't you?'

This was much too deep a question to be asked in a motorway service area on a hot day with lazy summer grooves blaring out of a car window in the next row of parking spaces. It felt so unreal, I couldn't even work out how I felt.

'I'm sorry,' I said. 'What are you going to do? You *are* going to wait till we get home, aren't you?'

'The book recommends that discipline be administered swiftly. It says that letting a lot of time pass reduces the effectiveness of the punishment. And I can see that. It pisses me off that the villains I catch don't go to trial for months on end. Makes me wonder if they even remember what they did by then, let alone feel guilt. But now I don't have to complain about the justice system. I *am* the justice system. And justice will be done.'

His smile was dazzling. You'd think I'd just given him a blowjob, rather than bickered over Whitesnake on the M3.

'Here?' I stammered, for clarification. 'In the car?'

I tried to imagine how that would be possible.

'No, not in the car. Come on. Let's go for a walk.'

He got out and opened my door for me.

Outside, the sun was fierce and I looked around at all the hot, grumpy, burger-eating people in the car park. What the hell did Dan have in mind? And could it be achieved in Burger King or WH Smith's?

Apparently not, because he took my hand and led me into the pine wood. A few picnic tables hosted families squabbling over food and squirrels lurking hopefully at their feet. There was a small swing park and beyond that – just trees and the soft, needle-strewn ground.

'You're seriously going to do this?'

Pine needles prickled my feet in their flip-flops. We were deeper in and the light was half-gone.

'Yes, seriously. And that's how you have to take me, Pip. Seriously.'

'I do.'

'No, you don't. You think of this as something you can do when you're in the mood. The rest of the time you can be as huffy and passive-aggressive – or aggressive-aggressive – as you like. No, Philippa. You're going to learn that this is going to be done wholeheartedly or not at all. You can't blow hot and cold with me.'

He stopped in a clearing. Even on this blazing hot day it was cold and forbidding there. When he turned to me, he looked so darkly intent that I was momentarily scared.

'That's not what I meant,' I said. 'I want you to be wholehearted. I want that. But ... this is a public place.'

He waved an arm.

'There's nobody here. We're far enough from the car park, so we won't be heard.'

'What if I scream blue murder?'

'What if you do?'

He patted his thigh.

'Come to me, Philippa.'

His lips were curling upwards and I had the distinct impression that he was more concerned with getting my cut-off jeans down than actual punishment. All the same, I felt that same set of contradictory tingles his stern face always triggered.

There was nothing for it. Neither fight nor flight was an option. Only surrender.

I wasn't sure how he meant to do this. There were no convenient tree stumps or logs for him to sit on, just row after row of spookily symmetrically arranged firs.

I went to stand before him and he pulled me against him, then pushed me into a bending position, bracing one of his arms beneath my stomach so that I was cinched around the waist by it. I could only see his back view and I tried to kick, to see if I could bring him to the ground, but his grip was firm enough to hold me in place.

'Keep still,' he warned, when I tried to reach for the nearest tree for something to hang on to.

The inability to see what he was doing or guess what would come next was intensely disorientating. Added to this was a nagging worry that somebody might stumble across us thus engaged.

Dan seemed to have no qualms, though, and his hand fell heavily on my tightly denim-covered bottom. The sound it made was loud and querulous, and so was the yelp that came from my mouth. He laid on more, punctuating each with a word.

'You.' Smack.

'Will.' Smack.

'Show.' Smack.

'Me.' Smack.

'More.' Smack.

'Respect.' Smack.

'Won't.' Smack.

'You?' Smack.

It seemed an answer was required.

'Yes,' I mewed. 'Oh, my God, someone's coming!'

They weren't. But the way Dan dropped me like a hot rock was enough to make me forget my sore bottom and roll around in the needles, cackling for joy.

'Fuck's sake, Pip!' he said, clutching his brow. 'You'll get me the sack.'

'Your face.' I laughed some more.

'You've asked for it,' he said, lunging for me.

We wrestled in the pine grove, shrieking and giggling,

until he had me pinned to the ground on my stomach, straddling my hips.

'Now you're for it,' he promised, reaching underneath to unbutton my shorts.

'Dan,' I whispered urgently. 'Somebody really might come.'

'Oh, yes,' he said gravely. 'Somebody might.'

I got more spanking on my thong-clad bare bottom, but it wasn't hard and by the time he'd warmed me, stranger danger was the last thing on my mind.

The first thing on my mind glided up inside me, the thong pulled rudely aside. I pushed my bottom back to help him get deeper, breathing in the forest scent and the smell of him on top.

'You don't get to wear shorts like that and make it through the journey unfucked,' he growled into my ear, thrusting hard.

I was very glad to hear it, and the tetchy tempers and impromptu punishments mutated into a glorious bone-melting shag.

I had needles stuck to my hands and knees, a stinging bum and a hot, sticky gusset for the rest of the motorway trip, but I was pretty happy with that. We listened to a CD we both liked and we were both in bloody good moods, all the way to the sea.

Which was where things went a bit wrong again.

I swear, that town is like Looking-Glass World. You

follow a sign for the town centre and find yourself on some arid stretch of suburban road, logjammed between massive retail parks.

Sans SatNav, we had to rely on the road map, and I'm not a big fan of road maps, especially when they are twelve years out of date and don't show which streets are one-way.

'Shit, where's that junction come from? It's not on the map.'

Dan made it to the other side of the traffic lights without a collision, but it was close enough.

'You said there was a roundabout there!'

'There … was. It's gone.'

'Look, where do I go now? Left or right?'

'Um, left, I think. Shit, no, that's a dead end. Bugger. Too late.'

This went on for a very long time. Neither of us was at fault exactly, but the combined effects of confusion and panic and being cooped up in a small, hot tin box burned our wicks right down to the fuses.

'For fuck's sake, *there. That way.*' I flapped my hand at a brown signpost perched precariously on a traffic island.

'There's no need to swear at me,' said Dan between gritted teeth. 'Next layby I see, I'm going to pull over, bend you over the bonnet and give that cane a good workout.'

'Shut up!'

'You don't think I'm serious? Try me.'

But before I could (although I was inclined not to), heaven arranged for a perfect view of the beach, the sea and the way down to it, and we concentrated our combined attention on achieving our mission of finding a parking space.

The sunshine and the blue surf evened out all rough edges of temper. We were there to have a good time, and we had it, lazing on the beach until it was time to find our friends for the promised barbecue party. The cane lay, neglected and forgotten, baking on the back seat.

Kez and Ginnie are friends of mine, dating back to a chaotic flatshare at university. They stayed down here in the sun, living the bohemian life, while I moved up to the city and met Dan. They always tease me that I'm their big sister, growing up and doing all the adult stuff like getting married and taking on a responsible job and mortgage while they still hang around bars picking up surfer dudes and smoking spliff into the early hours before going to their ever-changing jobs in art galleries and tapas bars and what have you. Kez is a vigorous member of the local alternative political scene while Ginnie is more an unreconstructed party girl. They both disapprove of Dan (whose presence will severely limit their drug consumption tonight) but put up with him for my sake.

'Time for me to say a little prayer,' said Dan, eyes fixed on the setting sun, having finally found a parking space in the district of winding hills and jumbled cottages in which my friends had made their home.

'Oh, don't. They like you.'

'They hate me. But they like you too much to show it.'

'Just smile and nod, smile and nod,' I said, the usual advice in these scenarios.

Dan sniffed the air as we got out of the car.

'Is that a home-grown blend I scent?'

'No, you knob, it's sausages.'

They didn't have much of a garden – just a tiny patch of walled-in gravel parallel to and behind the kitchen – but they had made the most of it, filling it with bunting and fairylights and all sorts while the barbecue smoked merrily in one corner. The kitchen and living room and hallway and stairs all heaved with bodies, so it was difficult at first to locate either Kez or Gin.

A few old faces, the names of which I'd mainly forgotten, appeared during the search. They greeted me effusively, then switched to guarded mode when they noticed Dan at my shoulder. Once we had passed, I kept feeling eyes boring into my back and hearing – though it was mostly my imagination – the words *She's the one that married the copper. That's him!*

Shifty looks and hands unconsciously patting pockets

and purses were the order of the day. The heavy, distinctively sweet smoke of weed wafted on the outside air, and I heard someone hiss, 'Put it out!' then Kez loomed in front of me, in a batik turban and massive earrings, smiling all over her face.

'Pip, wow, so good to see you again, how've you been?'

All my anxieties dissolved in her enthusiastic bear hug and I felt twenty-one again, ready for a night of red wine and flirting to heavy bass jams.

I stuck to the red wine, Dan not being a fan of flirtation with anyone but him. Ginnie, whose absence had been rather puzzling me, appeared at ten o'clock with a lank, limp-looking young man and an announcement, after which the reason for the party became clear.

She had gone and got herself engaged to the lank one – who described himself as an unemployed rock star but had an accent that suggested private schooling and a trust fund.

Champagne was drunk and dancing attempted, with much clashing of elbows, then most of the crowd melted away into clubland, leaving Kez, Ginnie, the unemployed rock star, Dan and me to hoover up what remained in the bottles.

'You never mentioned you were thinking of marriage,' I exclaimed, rounding on Ginnie with mock disapproval, though, after the amount I'd had, it might have sounded realler than I intended.

'Ah, you know,' she said with a fond smile at Rock Star (real name: Piers). 'It wasn't a plan. We were just messing around after a gig, had a few vodkas and, I dunno, Piers said wouldn't it be hilarious to see everyone's faces if we got married and ... we decided to do it.'

I worked to keep the smile on my face, but I think she must have seen something in my eyes because Piers took over the explanation, in defensive mode.

'Why, what better reasons are there? Why does anyone get married, anyway? It's just a fucking legal thing, a convention. A piece of paper.'

Oddly enough, he echoed some of my teenage clients during a debate I'd recently chaired on the relevance of marriage in the twenty-first century. They'd barely scraped together enough education to read, though, so they could be forgiven the unoriginality of the sentiment. From him, though, it grated.

'So that's why you're doing it?' said Dan. 'To see everyone's faces? And what about after that? After you've seen them and laughed?'

'I might have known you'd disapprove, PC Copper,' said Ginnie icily. 'Perhaps we don't want to embarrass you by being all loved-up and full of the grand passion. Not everyone's like that.'

She was having a dig at us. We had been pretty sickening in a Love's Young Dream kind of way when we met. I didn't see why I should feel ashamed about it though. At least our feelings for each other had been genuine and honest.

'You're in love though, right?' I asked, confused by the latent hostility in the air.

'Yeah, of course,' mumbled Piers, while Ginnie huffed and poured herself another glass.

'You know my feelings on the subject,' said Kez, giving me a sympathetic smile.

'Don't start, Kez. Nobody's forced me into this. Piers and I have an equal partnership. We going to make marriage mean whatever we want it to mean, so neither of us is perpetuating ancient oppressions.'

Both Kez and Ginnie gave Dan a daggers look, silently translated as *unlike him*.

'Unlike me,' said Dan, brightly but unhelpfully. 'I can't get enough oppressing, me. It's what I live for. I wake up every morning looking forward to another solid day of oppression. It keeps me young.'

'Dan.' I nudged him too hard and he spilled red wine on the carpet.

'Not everything's about you, Dan,' said Kez coldly. 'This is Gin and Piers' night. Don't try and turn the focus to yourself. Typical of you.' She spoke the last words in a mock undertone.

'Why are you having a go at Dan?' I wondered, only slightly drunkenly. 'Dan is a brilliant husband and an amazing advert for marriage. I say go for it, Ginnie.

Being married is fantastic. I've never regretted it and I bet I never will.'

Dan looked a little stunned, as if he thought I might have drunk far more than he'd realised.

'D'you mean that?' he said.

'Yeah, course I do.' I lurched towards him, puckering up. He obliged me with a kiss, if not the full-blooded snog I craved. 'You're fucking lush, you are. I love you so much, oh, my God, so much.'

'Yeah, I think perhaps the wine ... we ought to go to bed, maybe. C'mon, soldier. Let's get a pint of water to take up with us.'

He'd stood and was pulling me up by my elbow, but all around us a cacophony of protest seemed to form a circle, unintelligible but no less vehement for that.

'Who do you think you are, telling her to go to bed?'

'She's a grown woman, she can make her own decisions.'

'Tell him to piss off, Pip. He's not the boss of you.'

I knew that they just wanted Dan to go to bed so they could skin up in peace. I'd told them numerous times that Dan would turn a blind eye just so long as they didn't try to get him to smoke, but they seemed convinced that he was looking for any excuse to clap them in irons, so they continued in their obstinate practice.

'Look,' I said unsteadily. 'I'm sick of this. As far as I'm concerned, Dan's proved himself the right man for me over and over again, but you won't hear a word in his favour. I'm sick of the way you treat him and I'm sick of being pitied and fussed over as if I'm some kind of … oh, forget it. I'm not staying. I'm leaving. Let's find a hotel. Good luck with married life, eh?'

I made a dramatic exit, slightly marred by tripping over a stray ashtray, and ran out into the street, a storm of blether at my heels. I think Dan was behind me. I hoped he was.

I got to the car and realised I didn't have any keys and turned to look for him.

But Kez had given chase first and was jogging up behind me, entreating me to wait and come back and listen and nobody had meant it that way and it was all a misunderstanding …

More phrases of this nature were pouring from her lips when she chanced to look in at the back window of the car.

She stopped short and uttered a small scream.

The lights in the upstairs windows of two cottages went on.

'What the fuck's that for?' she demanded, pointing at the back seat.

At first I couldn't think what she meant, but then the Cabernet fog cleared a little and I remembered what was in there. Oh.

'What?' I stalled for time.

'That! A cane. Like they used to have in schools in Victorian times.'

'More recently than that, actually, it wasn't abolished formally until nineteen –'

'Whatever!' she shrieked.

She seemed to remember where she was then and lowered her tone to a confidential murmur.

'Oh, God, Pip, please tell me … look, there's a place for you whenever you need it … let me find the number of the local shelter for you … Is it because he's a cop? You feel you can't get out of it? It'll be OK, Pip, I swear. I'll get my group behind you. We'll all stand beside you. I'll blog about it.'

It was only then that I realised the assumption she was making.

And she was right, even though she was also atrociously wrong.

And I had no idea how to even begin to explain. Indeed, my explanations would probably only make things sound very much worse.

'No, Kez, no, you've got the wrong end of the, uh, well, the stick, so to speak.'

'Are you telling me he doesn't beat you? I need the truth, Pip. The truth.'

'The truth is, it's a, um, a kink. Fetish. You know.'

'He doesn't beat you?'

Christ, she was tenacious.

'Nothing happens that nobody wants,' I said obliquely.

'The snivelling little git,' she said, suddenly alight with a different variety of indignation. 'He makes you dress up for him, doesn't he?'

'Oh, well ... now and again.'

'Don't tell me. PVC, leather, thigh-high boots. I've heard that men in positions of unwarranted power like to pretend to relinquish it to women they pay. Or women who can't say no to them. Like their wives.'

'Well, that's ... not quite it ...'

'Oh, I don't want to hear the details, Pip. God. He makes you whip him, does he? Kisses your feet and all that?'

I had no idea what to say now. I was at sea and adrift. Kez had made her supposition and it was less dangerous to me than the other one, so I suppose I just ... let her go with it.

'It's OK, Kez, we're both one hundred per cent cool with what we do. We're happy. We're well matched.'

She stared at me.

'You like hurting him?'

'I like what he likes.'

'Christ, you're so co-dependent. I despair of you. But look. I wanted to say, come back in.'

'I'm not going anywhere my husband isn't welcome.'

'It's OK.'

Dan's voice. He was behind Kez on the pavement, in company with Ginnie and Piers.

'Dan.'

'Come on, we can't go anywhere now,' he reasoned. 'I've had a drink and so have you. Let's just go to bed and everything will be better in the morning.'

'But don't you mind?'

'As long as we're welcome …' He looked at Kez and Ginnie, who both offered a shamefaced nod.

'All right then. But I'm serious.' I wagged a not-very-steady finger at my old friends. 'Love me, love my cop.'

Somehow we all made it back into the house without falling over, until I fell into bed. A futon, to be precise, on the first-floor landing, but anything would do at that point.

Ginnie and Piers cooked brunch the next day (I can't really say morning) and we all sat around the table speaking to each other with exaggerated courtesy, except when the other three stopped to exchange meaningful looks, or Kez muttered stuff under her breath about sexual servitude and marriage being slavery.

It was quite horrible and I was glad to get away.

'What was all that about?' Dan wondered aloud, once we were safely back on the motorway.

'What? Kez and Gin being idiots?'

'All those weird comments. Have you told them something? You haven't, have you? No wonder they hate my bloody guts. Jesus, Pip.'

'I didn't! I didn't tell them … what you think.'

'Philippa.' He looked away from the road for long enough to give me a goosebump-inducing hard stare.

'I might have twisted the truth a little,' I admitted.

'Tell me now. Services are ten miles away. If you want me to use the facilities again ...'

'No! I was trying to protect you. You can't punish me for that.'

'OK, so explain. What did you say?'

'I might have let Kez believe a conclusion she jumped to. I didn't say it myself.'

'Stop covering your arse, my dear. You know it's futile when I'm around.'

I blushed and felt a burning between my thighs.

'She saw the cane in the back seat. I didn't know what to say. I let her make up her own mind about it, and her own mind came up with an interesting alternative explanation.'

'Which was?'

'That it's me who canes you.'

'Oh, God.' He laughed out loud for quite a while. 'I think I'm going to need those services after all.'

'It's not my fault!'

'No, no, I'm not blaming you. You couldn't have done much else under the circumstances. It was a smart move to let her carry on thinking that.'

'I thought she might try and report you for assault or something if she knew the truth. We know why we do what we do, but it's quite hard to explain to someone on the outside. I just didn't know where to start. So I didn't start.'

'And why should you? It's our private life, babe. None of her business. But oh, dear.' He chuckled again. 'I'm just picturing myself in tight rubber trunks and a gimp mask. Not my style at all.'

'Hmm, the gimp mask, no, but tight rubber trunks …'

'Don't go there. Unless you'd like a pair. Tiny little shiny rubber hotpants. What do you say?'

'Uncomfortable.'

'Exactly.'

Oh, no. Now I could see his mind whirring down a new path. Canes, butt plugs and now rubber. All I'd asked for was a bit of spanking. But I seemed to have created a kinky monster.

'Anyway,' I said, anxious to redirect him from this particular route. 'The point is, I saved your bacon, so you should be grateful to me. And by "grateful" I mean gearing up for cooking me dinner followed by giving me a full body massage. Don't you think?'

He conceded this point and we had a lovely post-hangover evening of smooching and snacking on the sofa before the scented oils came out.

'So,' he said as I lay beneath him in bed, my legs wrapped around his waist while he thrust slowly and rhythmically inside me. 'You made me into your submissive. I feel I need to redress the balance. How shall I do it?'

'Mmm,' I said, grinding my hips to increase the friction. I was in no mood for a discussion. 'Fuck me.'

'I already am.' He sped up to illustrate the point. 'But I feel the need to reassert myself within the relationship. Show you I'm not your whipping boy.'

'You know it,' I gasped. 'Oh, God, right there.'

He'd put his finger on my clitoris and I jerked upwards to meet the pressure.

'Are you going to come for me?' he whispered.

It wasn't too long before I did, twisting beneath him while he pounded into me, preparing to lose control.

'Mmm, you like that, don't you?' he panted. 'But wait until tomorrow. I'm going to give you something to remember.'

The thought of it obviously excited him, because he spilled straightaway, his face stretched into a mask of rapture.

'What?' I yawned, enjoying the limp weight of him on top of me before he began to crush the breath from my body. 'What are you going to give me?'

'Wait and see.'

The three worst words in the English language.

7 *August*

He wouldn't give me any kind of clue over breakfast, though he did bring the cane in from the car in a manner I'd describe as ostentatious. Or even threatening.

'Don't keep me in suspense,' I begged, but he shook his head and waved the damn thing at me.

'Suspense is good for you,' he said. 'Concentrates the mind.'

'What shift are you on today?'

'I'm back at nine. Don't worry about cooking for me. I'll grab something at the canteen before I leave.'

'I won't be able to eat,' I said, with woeful visage. 'I'll be too nervous.'

'If you don't eat, you know what happens,' he said.

I felt a strange sense-memory twinge of the buttocks.

Yes. I knew that all right.

As it went, I didn't feel tense at work at all. I felt excited, the way I used to before a big date before we were married. After all, this wasn't real punishment. It was fun kinkiness with a pretendy layer of punishment on top. Perhaps that was what I wanted all along, and the 'for your own good' stuff had been the precursor. I wouldn't have enjoyed it, or felt half the thrill of anticipation, though, if I didn't have the experience and the undertone of 'real' punishment. 'Let's play whipping tonight' just wouldn't have worked for me – and yet that was what this was, essentially.

I had plenty of time to wonder what would happen when he got home.

I picked at a baked potato and flicked between TV channels, but nothing went in – mouth or brain, really.

I tried to get The Book back out of its box file, but it wasn't there any more. Dan had re-hidden it, which was a bit stable door and bolting horse, but it still annoyed me. I wanted to reread some of it, for preparation.

I didn't know what to wear and texted him after washing the few dishes.

'Your short PJs will do,' he texted back. 'Wait for me in the bedroom.'

I found The Book in his bedside drawer once I'd changed into the cotton short pyjamas. He had a book-mark in it. It was the chapter on Anal Discipline.

I shut it quickly and took a few breaths.

Just because he was reading that chapter, it didn't mean he was going to do anything about it. Did it?

I clenched my sphincter and tried to get involved in reading my own book, but I couldn't possibly concentrate and the same sentence tried unsuccessfully to hammer its way into my brain over and over again.

I was no closer to processing the words when I heard the key in the lock.

My heart began to thunder and my ears to roar. I put the book down then picked it back up again, trying to look natural.

Be relaxed, I told myself. Be casual. He won't expect it.

He came into the room, looking slightly crumpled after a long shift on a hot day, with rolled-up shirtsleeves and a pinkish tinge to his skin.

'Hi,' I said. I tried to sound nonchalant, not sure it came off.

'Well, good evening,' he said, folding his arms and raising an eyebrow. 'Could we have the book down, please?'

'Since you're asking nicely,' I said pertly, placing it on the bedside table.

His eyebrows crept higher.

'And if I didn't?' he asked with deceptive politeness.

I felt the delicious danger prickle at my skin.

I shrugged, sniggering self-consciously, like a kid caught passing notes in class.

'Lie down on your stomach,' he said.

I had been expecting more banter before business so I didn't react straightaway, until he took a step closer to me and then I threw myself face down on the duvet, hiding in its clean, comfortable folds.

'So,' he said, and the mattress groaned under his weight. He straddled me, his knees either side of my thighs, my legs pressed down. 'I'm your bitch, am I?'

'No,' I giggled.

'But that's what your friends think I am. Your friends think that I crawl around this flat on my hands and knees in tight leather shorts, until you decide to take them down and thrash my arse. Don't they?'

'Maybe something like that,' I mumbled.

'Yeah, maybe something like that. Do you know what I think you should do? I think you should call them up on the phone later on and describe some of the things that I've done to you. Do you think that's fair?'

'Depends what you do,' I said. 'What are you going to do?'

'I haven't made my final decision yet,' he said. 'But you can be fairly sure that these aren't going to be necessary.'

He yanked down the pyjama shorts, raising himself up for a moment so that they could rest around my knees.

I yelped and tried to wriggle out from under him, but he clamped his legs tight around me and smacked his hand down on my bare bum.

'You're going to keep still, Pip,' he said. 'And behave yourself. Aren't you?'

'I'll try.'

Another smack.

'I need a bit more commitment than that,' he warned.

'I'll be good,' I promised. 'But what are you going to do?'

'Something I've been thinking of doing for years. But somehow never had the confidence to suggest. Until now.'

'Why now?'

'I'm not worried you'll think I'm a disgusting pervert any more. You know I am.'

'That's for sure.'

'Good. So you won't be too shocked by what I'm about to do to you.'

He got off me and began rummaging in his work bag, which he'd dropped by the side of the bed. I twisted my neck to watch him. His face was redder. He was still a *little* bit nervous, for all his bravado. I wanted to hold his hand and tell him it would be OK. How absurd – *what* would be OK? I didn't even know.

His hand emerged from the bag wrapped around a small squeezy bottle full of colourless gel. He put it down and I read the label. 'Slide-a-ride'. It was a lubricant.

We'd never used lube before because, well, I usually didn't need any assistance in that department. Dan only had to look at me a certain way for my knickers to flood.

So ...

He reached into the bag again and pulled out a rectangular cardboard and cellophane presentation package, of the kind you might get a set of bath products wrapped in at Christmas. Except there were no body lotions or bath salts in this box.

No, there were three pink, strange-shaped objects. They reminded me a bit of the ornate handles at the bottom of my grandmother's bathroom light pull switches – flared for a more comfortable grip. But I knew that the flaring was nothing to do with ease of wrapping fingers around. And I knew what these babies were. I'd seen them in The Book. They were butt plugs.

'Oh, my God,' I exclaimed, unable to stop myself. 'Are you serious?'

He sat on the side of the bed and held my face, looking at me in a manner that made it perfectly clear that he was.

It wasn't just my heart fluttering. Everything was in turmoil and I could scarcely identify my responses. Sometimes they seemed broadly positive, and then the lurch in my stomach begged to disagree and I thought I was dead against the whole idea.

'I want to do this,' he said softly. 'Not to terrorise or punish you at all, but to see if you like it. I've always secretly wanted to, well, I won't pussyfoot around, take you up the arse. But I don't want the first time to be painful or shocking for you. So I thought this ...'

I exhaled. 'Right. Oh.' I didn't know what to say. It seemed beyond the pale to admit that I found the idea quite exciting. Surely I should resist the idea with every fibre of my being? But then, I was happy for him to give me a sore bottom in the other way. So this seemed a natural step to take.

'And perhaps we could make it part of the routine, you know, instead of spanking, or in addition. I think –' his voice became almost a whisper '– I'd like that.'

He looked as if he might salivate. My bared pussy began to flood at the thought of what he'd been planning and fantasising. He wanted to do unspeakable things to me. I wanted to let him.

But I didn't want him to know I wanted it.

My head might have exploded, if only my lower parts weren't so insistent in their needs.

What should I do? If I said, 'Yeah, OK, go for it,' I'd lose the best part of the excitement. Pretend to protest and hope he'd do it anyway? Be so over the top that he'd realise I was play-acting? I couldn't expect him to read my mind, but I didn't want my mind read. I wanted to be told what to do and made to accept it.

For a moment, we simply looked at each other and a chasm of real fear seemed to separate us.

Then I said, 'You're the boss.'

He smiled and took several deep breaths. Sweat had broken out on his forehead and he wiped it away.

'OK then,' he said, picking up the box.

'In here,' I whispered swiftly, to clarify. 'In this room, you're the boss.'

'Except when you misbehave, my dear,' he reminded me, wincing as he tried to rip off the sellotape using only his finger.

'You need scissors.'

'I don't need scissors. Don't tell me what to do. I'm the boss, remember. Shit. I need scissors.'

I laughed as he loped off to the kitchen to find some, then took up the package in my hands to investigate further.

The three plugs were of different sizes. I presumed I was only in for the most miniature of them today. All the same, it looked … alien. Yes, like an alien, a tiny pink fleshy thing. I supposed it was made of latex and would feel rubbery and cold. A little rubbery cold thing intended to prepare me for … a big, fleshy, hot thing. It hardly seemed appropriate.

The thought crashed over me again. Dan wanted to bugger me. He was going to do it. I was going to feel what it was like to have his hard, thick cock right inside my tight back passage. Maybe not today, but sometime soon.

Gulp.

He came back with the scissors and cut the tape off the box flap.

'Ready?' he asked softly, removing the plastic tray with its three inhabitants. Big, medium-sized and small. I couldn't help thinking of the three bears. Goldilocks was really going to have her work cut out tonight.

'As I'll ever be,' I said. I'd buried my face in the duvet again. I wasn't going to be able to face him until his … dabblings … were over. At least he couldn't really ask me to – my neck wouldn't allow it. Thank goodness for rears being at the rear.

'OK then. Relax and hold still.'

He straddled me again and spent a little time kneading between my shoulder blades, loosening my knots, until I was sighing and floating.

'Keep everything nice and relaxed,' he murmured, shifting down a little for readier access to my bottom.

I heard him shake the bottle then a tiny glug as he poured a little lubricant out.

I waited. I couldn't help but tense a little.

I flinched when his cold, lubed finger prodded its way between my cheeks. He held them open with his other hand, stroking the skin with his thumb until I'd stopped wriggling.

'The more relaxed you are, the better this will be,' he assured me. 'Sink into the mattress, love. Let your bones rest.'

Somehow his voice combined with the gentle stroking of his thumb began to exert a hypnotic effect and I stopped bucking when his lubricated finger delved deeper, burrowing down towards that tiny aperture.

He circled it, lower and slower, moving in towards his target in infinitesimal degrees. He took so long in this considerate priming that I began to move from anxious to turned on. There was definitely a pleasurable sensation building, rather to my surprise. And I felt so small and helpless, like a patient on a table with a doctor who knew what was best for me and would brook no argument. I was seeing it all now. I was meant to be submissive.

A rebel voice inside me still insisted, *This is outrageous, he can't do this to you*, but guilt was going to have be deferred. Guilt and shame and all those things ... How topsy-turvy it all was. You were supposed to be punished because you were guilty of wrong-doing. You were supposed to feel shame for what you had done. And here I was, feeling guilty and ashamed because I wanted the punishment.

What had gone wrong inside me, that I felt this way?

Was it wrong at all?

What was right?

I no longer knew, but I did care. Just not right now. Not while Dan was pushing the tip of a finger into the tiny forbidden ring, making me gasp and flinch.

131

'How's that?' he whispered.

'Just so strange,' I replied.

I wasn't able to explain it. It didn't hurt as such and it wasn't a blissfully pre-orgasmic feeling either. It was just ... different. Physically, it wasn't that amazing, but mentally it took me in its tight embrace and whisked me away into a place where I was absolutely dominated. I could think of nothing else but what was being done to me.

He didn't rush. The finger made a very slow, very exploratory foray inside. From the initial breach to knuckle-deep seating probably took a good five minutes. I felt that I was being tested and I made sure he knew if he hurt me or gave me pleasure. I owed him this honesty.

'OK,' he said, twisting his finger this way and that, making my stomach flutter in a kind of panic. 'I think you can take it.'

If the entry of his finger had felt strange, it was nothing compared to its exit. I felt as if he was pulling part of me out with it and my muscles weren't happy. They tensed around him, as if they wanted him for a prisoner.

'Keep relaxed,' he admonished, leaving me empty.

But not for long.

'This won't feel the same,' he told me, unnecessarily.

'I think I knew that,' I said.

'Do you think you're in a good position to get sarcastic with me, Pip?'

He jiggled the end of the plug between my cheeks. My muscles contracted and I sucked in air at its coldness.

'Uh, no.'

'Right. Now, hold on. I'm going in.'

Oh, this was a different proposition to his finger entirely! The blunt tip opened me up but, instead of maintaining that comfortable level of accessibility, the plug made me stretch and stretch some more, until my eyes were watering.

'Oh, ow, this stings!' I complained, twisting my hips this way and that.

He put a hand on the small of my back, keeping me still.

'It'll pass,' he soothed. 'The widest part is in now. All you have to do is accept the rest.'

He was right; the rest of it slid in with comparative ease. In fact, it felt as if I was pulling it in of my own accord, even though I wasn't. A pat on my bottom to make sure the flat end was properly wedged between my cheeks made it clear that I was now fully and completely plugged.

Now it was all the way in, it wasn't terribly uncomfortable. But it was hard to ignore the feeling of it, a hard and remorseless presence inside my most private space. I could see why it was recommended as a punishment. And this was the smallest one!

'Tell me how you feel,' said Dan, massaging my bum cheeks. Every time he drew them apart with his big hands, my muscles clenched around the plug, as if worried it would sink deeper inside me. It made me squirm. The squirming made me aware of how wet my pussy was. What I wanted now, right now, was for Dan to fuck me. The feeling of fullness was all-absorbing and addictive – I wanted to be fuller. I wanted more.

But Dan didn't rip off his trousers and oblige.

Instead he climbed off me and went to sit on the pillows, his back to the wall.

He slapped his thigh.

'Come on, missy, over my knee,' he said.

'Ohhh … really?' I wheedled.

'Yes, really. You need to know what it feels like to be spanked with one of those inside you. More to the point, *I* need to know. I'm finessing my techniques. I haven't decided whether I should do plugs before or after spankings. You're helping me with my research. Come on.'

I was genuinely curious, too, to know what dimension the plug would add, so I crawled over his thighs. Every move kept me conscious of the invader at my rear, but no position made it more conspicuous than being over Dan's lap with my bottom raised and my legs apart, as ordered.

I couldn't face him. I was far too embarrassed. He

knew what was in me – he had put it there. And he knew I was getting a form of pleasure from it, or I would be putting up a fight. He knew, in short, exactly what kind of sick pervert I was.

At least the spanking distracted me from my mortification. In a way, the pain – crisp and sharp and clean – made me feel better. But it wasn't long before I began to understand how the plug altered the sensation. As the smacks became harder, they sent a quake down inside me, resulting in a series of pangs that spread outwards around the plug and through my bottom. I was being punished inside and out. The plug jiggled constantly and I knew it was getting me wetter than ever.

Dan knew it too. He must have known from the way I bucked and moaned, and if that hadn't given the game away, it was clear when he put the knuckles of his free hand up against my clit. He continued to spank with one hand and rub up and down between my pussy lips with the other at the same time. It meant he had to use his unaccustomed arm for the spanking and the strokes were a little lighter and clumsier than I was used to. But the stroking made up for it, oh, yes, how it made up for it.

Any self-control I had was slipping away, rising up from the crown of my head like steam. I clung to the duvet, then clawed at Dan's leg, bumping and grinding into his knuckles.

'You're going to come, aren't you?' he said, as if it were inevitable.

It was.

I came with my bum hot and spanked, my back passage plugged up, my husband's fist pressing into my soaked pussy lips and swollen clit. I was so blown apart by the intensity of it that I started to cry.

'No, no, no, no,' whispered Dan, rearranging me into a tight embrace and kissing the tears. 'Don't cry, please, I didn't mean to …'

'It's all right,' I said, getting a wisp of sense back into my head. 'It's good. Just a bit too good … you know?'

He sighed with relief.

'Right. You're sure? You're OK?'

'Much more than OK.'

'Good. Because I really, really want to fuck you now.'

'You mean …?'

Was he going to do IT?

He shook his head.

'I'm building up to it. But I'm going to leave the plug in. I want you to feel what it's like to be double-stuffed.'

Hmm, well, in the interests of science, I supposed I could go along with that.

'You're sure you're OK?' he fussed, kissing me again.

I nodded.

'Take me, officer.'

136

His wicked smile chased away the anxiety lines around his eyes.

'You asked for it.'

I found myself forthwith upon all fours, thighs wide, plug still making its presence known at my rear.

Dan made short work of his clothes, then his hands were on my shoulders, his thighs flush against mine, his cock warm and hard between my pussy lips, bathing in their juices.

'Mm, lovely red bum,' he said appreciatively, stroking the heated skin with one hand. 'I hate not being able to fuck you after I've punished you. I always want a piece of that red arse. Oh, God.'

He pushed me down between my shoulder blades so that my face was low and my bottom as high as could be, then he was inside me, so quickly and effortlessly that I yelped.

He kept one hand firmly on my hip, the other on my shoulder, so all I could do was take the thrusts and try not to crumple in a heap on the bed. Such thrusts, powerful and strong, each one a jolt.

'I'm ... going ... deep,' he panted. 'You're ... getting ... it ... hard.'

Didn't I know it?

I moaned and whimpered into the duvet, feeling the extra sensation every time his cock tip glanced against the tip of the butt plug. I had never realised how close the two passages were, but it seemed that only a very thin barrier separated them.

The double penetration was exquisite and, even though I had come so recently and so hard, the friction struck sparks of new arousal very quickly.

'I can see your plug,' he muttered, still fucking me as if his life depended on it. 'I can see it inside your arse. I can feel it against my cock. You need it. You love it, don't you?'

'Yes, yes.'

I could barely keep my limbs in position now. I was streaming with sweat and my bones wanted to collapse. If I shook any more violently, my teeth would fall out.

'God! Yes!' he roared, giving my bum a hearty smack as he rode into his climax. He fell on top of me, squashing the breath from me, but didn't pull out.

I was grateful for this. I hadn't quite reached my own orgasm and wondered if a little bit of wriggling underneath him might just ...

He knew what I was doing and he slipped his hand beneath his stomach and my bottom and began playing with the plug, making the flange move around in a circle, while I ground my hips and pushed back against his still-hard cock.

'Once wasn't enough, eh, greedy girl?' he murmured into my hair.

I flushed but wasn't ashamed enough to stop now. I

was going to get that orgasm and nothing else mattered.

Half a minute of jerking and bucking got me there, huffing into the duvet, enjoying the solid weight of my husband and the way it restricted my movements.

'That's it,' I said after a minute or so more. 'I'm dead.'

'I hope not,' he said, rolling off me. 'I couldn't do without you.'

We drifted swiftly into a snooze and didn't really revive until we were in the shower together a couple of hours later.

'That was a valuable exercise,' said Dan, soaping my bum. He had pulled out the plug while I knelt on all fours on the bathroom rug. It had been the most humiliating part of the whole experience and I side-eyed it as it rested in soapy water in the washbasin, taunting me from afar.

My bottom felt a little sore, inside and out, but that was probably more to do with falling asleep with the plug inserted than anything else. I should remember not to do that in future.

In future.

That meant that I accepted that butt plugs were going to be part of my life. It was a done deal. No going back.

'Valuable?' I said with a yawn. 'Why valuable?'

'I learned that there's no point spanking you with a plug in unless I want you to get wildly turned on. I'll have to leave the plugs for afterwards. When you're in the corner, maybe. Or use them separately, without spanking you at all. Hmm. I wonder ...

'I don't like the sound of this wondering. What are you plotting?'

'That's for me to know,' he said, parting my bum cheeks and dripping shower gel between them, 'and you to find out.'

'When will I find out?'

'Behave yourself and perhaps you never will.'

'You make me want to be bad, just so I can find out.'

He grinned and kissed my neck, smoochy and slow.

'I dare you,' he said.

28 August

I know it's been a long time without a diary entry – three weeks – but we went away for a fortnight in the sun and all domestic discipline arrangements were deferred while I read blockbusters on sunbeds, sampled every different cocktail on the menu and tried to fend off Dan, who seemed obsessed with the idea of having sex on the beach. Not for me. The sand, ugh.

My natural tetchiness only lasted a couple of days after touchdown and for the rest of the holiday I was as relaxed as a cat stretched out on a sunny patio. Dan really had nothing to reproach me with, and besides, the Mediterranean climate didn't seem suited to rules and routines. I expect it's all in my head, but I think of all that as being a northern European thing.

It had been hot in town before we left, but heat at home is different. It means sweating in your work clothes, polluted air, stinking bins on collection day. It makes everything more stressful.

Lucky, then, that on the day we landed at Gatwick the British summer was well and truly over and we ran from the terminal to the car park through a gauntlet of hailstones.

And now, on Bank Holiday Monday, weather conditions were no better, which boded badly for the barbecue we'd been invited to by one of Dan's police mates.

It'd been weird since we got back from Spain, as if one of us was waiting for the other to bring up the subject of our dodgy pre-holiday activities, but nobody wanted to be the one to break the silence. The two weeks away seemed to have re-set us back to our defaults. Me snappy. Him sighing. The odd silent stand-off, a few instances of under-the-breath muttering and passive aggression. I was creeping slowly back into my old, unwanted ways.

I didn't want to go to the barbecue much and I did my hair and make-up grudgingly, wishing I could stay home and watch TV instead. After all, it was back to work tomorrow and I didn't want to be drinking and staying out late. I was already in a mood of high dudgeon by the time I got into the car.

'We aren't staying late, are we?' I griped as Dan turned the key in the ignition.

'No, no, not late. I can't drink anyway, since I'm driving ... unless you want to ...'

'Drive home? Oh. OK.'

There were advantages to this course. I could leave when I wanted, as the designated driver, instead of waiting for Dan to finish an interminable round of cop anecdotes. They were good anecdotes, but I'd heard them all before.

And I wouldn't risk a hangover. I know it's easy to intend to stick to no more than two alcoholic drinks, alternate them with water, blah blah, but somehow two often seem to stretch to more, especially when people refill your glass without asking.

'Really?' Dan stared at me, delaying putting his foot on the accelerator. 'You're sure? Even though we have to go through Smash-Up Junction?'

'Well, it should be OK later on at night. It won't exactly be rush hour.'

'Cool. Thanks, love.'

Dan was chipper as he guided us through Bank Holiday traffic to his friend's place on the other side of town.

He lived in an apartment complex with an underground car park – the barbecue was on his roof terrace. At least, that was the idea, but the driving rain forced us all indoors and he had to make use of the oven instead.

I turned down all offers of wine and beer and stuck to Coke. These dos were even more boring without alcohol, though, and I couldn't really join in with all the shop talk that was going on. I had to content myself with over-eating and smiling indulgently at Dan's stories. Perhaps I should have brought a book.

After two hours of this, I suggested that perhaps we should go home.

There was a chorus of protest, in which Dan joined.

'We've only just got here.'

I think he was on his third can of lager, or it might have been his fourth. He was at that stage where he wanted to hold forth to an avid audience, and delight in his eloquence and popularity. Two more cans and he'd be telling everyone how much he loved them.

I'm sure I'm just as annoying when drunk, but it's nails down a blackboard to watch this kind of behaviour when you're sober.

'It's a work night,' I said, as calmly as I could.

'For you,' he said. 'I'm on nights tomorrow and Wednesday. C'mon, another hour won't hurt.'

'Fine,' I said, in my best 'I mean the opposite of fine' voice.

I left the group and went into the kitchen.

If I had any more Coke I'd turn into a gibbering, bug-eyed caffeine freak.

One glass of wine. Not enough to take me over the limit.

I knew Dan strongly disapproved of drinking anything before driving, but I figured one wouldn't

144

hurt. He wouldn't know, being beered up to the gills himself.

I poured myself a Pinot Grigio – because it wouldn't give me a purple tongue, never accuse me of having no talent for crime – and sat myself on one of the barstools at the kitchen counter. I took down a cookery book from the shelf and began to read as I sipped.

About ten minutes into this, one of the female cops from Dan's division whom I vaguely knew came in and started chatting about recipes. The chat sort of drew me in, and by the time I realised she'd poured me another, I'd half-drunk it.

Shit. Now I was over the limit.

It was all Dan's fault! Why did he have to stay another hour? Pure selfishness!

As was my old habit, I was converting my anger at myself into anger at him, but I couldn't see it at the time. I was blinded with righteous wrath and wine.

I put down my glass and went back into the main living area. Hearty male laughter rang out from the corner sofa where Dan and his mates were settled.

As I entered, Dan looked up, put down his empty can and half-rose to his feet. He fell back, precipitating another gale of laughter.

'Oops,' he said. 'Ready to go, my angel?' he asked, putting his hand over his mouth to suppress a burp. Yep. Drunk as a skunk.

'If I'm an angel already, yes, definitely,' I said, to chuckles.

I didn't want to confess my crime in front of all these people, though.

I waited until Dan had done all his elaborate goodbye rituals, slung a slightly clumsy arm around my shoulder and made his way to the lifts.

'Good party,' he said, obviously making a massive effort not to slur. So he wasn't that far gone. 'D'you enjoy yourself, babe?'

'Er, yeah. Maybe a bit too much.'

He gave me a puzzled look as we stepped out into the basement car park.

'Whass that?'

'The thing is …'

We arrived by the car. There was nobody else around.

'I can't drive back.'

'Oh, Pip, you promised. Look at me. I can't.'

'I had a drink. Two drinks.'

This seemed to sober him like a fingersnap between the eyes.

'You did what?'

'I know, but I was bored. And you were getting drunk. I'd had too much Coke. And I only meant to have the one …'

'Philippa, one is too many. You know how I feel about that. How many times have I told you about the fatal accidents I've had to attend, thanks to some twat thinking they're cleverer than the drink-drive laws? Eh? I can't believe you'd ...'

'I know, I know, I only meant to have one ...'

'That's what they all say.'

'Yeah, but I'm not getting in the car, am I? I'd never do that.'

'Damn right you're not. Jesus. I can't believe you'd do this. I'm ... right. OK. This is the perfect example of when I should ...' He paused and took a breath. 'Bend over the bonnet.'

'What? No!'

'Do as you're told, Philippa. I'm very disappointed in you tonight.'

I looked back at the lift door and took another desperate scan of the car park. It was deserted. And something in Dan's eyes made me feel the impossibility of defying him.

'What if someone comes?' I asked in a very small voice.

'Then I'll stop. I'm only going to give you a taste of what's to come. I want to sober up before I deal with this properly. But the book says punishment is more effective when it's immediate. So ... please ...'

I could hardly believe I was going along with this, but I turned away from him and rested my elbows on the dusty bonnet of the car. It needed a wash, I thought irrelevantly. I traced a pattern in the dust, thinking of the filthy white van that used to be parked up our road in the grime of which some knob had written, 'I wish my wife was as dirty as this.'

I yelped out a plea when he lifted up my skirt to reveal my knickers.

'Must you? This is a public place.'

'If you can't do the time, love, don't do the crime,' he advised.

I felt the cool air of the basement chamber settle on my thighs and the exposed parts of my bottom. It combined with the slight wine haze to form a sensual cocktail that was much more sexy than I expected it to be.

Suddenly, I was looking forward to the first stroke.

Until it landed, loud and sharp, on my poor bum. My knickers were no protection at all, pathetic stretch lace numbers that served only to hold the sting in and increase the heat.

'Don't,' said Dan, smacking a second time.

'Drink.'

'Ow!'

'And.'

'Stop it.'

'Drive.'

'I didn't!'

'Unrepentant?' he asked dangerously.

'No, I'm sorry. I wish I hadn't had the wine.'

'Just.'

'Argh!'

'Say.'

'Oh, that hurts.'

'No.'

'I will! I did. I tried to.'

Another voice added to our fraught debate.

'Is everything all right here?'

A middle-aged man in a blue uniform stood by the lift door.

I shot up and rubbed my bottom, hiding behind Dan.

'Fine,' he said.

'You realise these premises are monitored by CCTV?'

'Oh ... no. We didn't.'

'So I gather. Perhaps you should go home, eh? These things are best kept private.' He gave Dan a mortifying little wink.

Even worse, while this conversation was ongoing, one of Dan's friends appeared, jingling his car keys.

'You all right, Danno?' he asked, looking after the concierge as he lumbered back off to his secret den of cameras.

'Yeah, just found out Twinkletoes here is over the limit. Going to have to call a cab and pick the car up tomorrow.'

'Don't call me that,' I hissed.

He always called me that in front of his friends. It drove me mad.

149

'I'll give you a lift,' offered the friend. I think his name was Patrick. 'Sears Corner, isn't it?'

'Yeah. Would you?'

'It's on my way.'

'You're a star, mate. C'mon, *Twink*. Let's make the best of a bad situation.'

I sat in the back seat, feeling the burn from the spanking, while Dan went in the front, beside his friend.

'Designated driver forgot her designation, eh?' said Patrick jovially, reversing out of the space.

'I didn't mean to,' I muttered.

'So what did the attendant guy want?'

'Oh, nothing, just wondered why we were hanging around in the car park without getting into the car.'

'Really?' Patrick left a question mark in the air, as if he knew more.

'What, do you think I'm lying?' Dan sounded slightly aggressive, the beers returning in full effect.

'Blimey, Dan, you sound like one of our suspects. I was just wondering if you realised that there's a live stream to the car-park CCTV on Jim's laptop.'

I saw Dan's shoulders tense and I bit my lip, not daring to react. Had we been seen?

A long beat of silence ended with Dan saying, 'Seriously?' in a low tone.

'Look, it's none of my business what you get up to in your –'

'Who saw us? How many of them?'

'It was just me. I was looking at some photos of Jim's rock-climbing holiday last month, wanted to see if it was something I'd go for. Got bored and started fiddling around with stuff. Found the car-park cam and ...'

'Yeah, yeah, busted,' said Dan resignedly. 'Keep it to yourself, yeah?'

'Of course.' He took a quick look back at me. 'You're OK, Phil?'

'God, yes.'

'You're sure?'

Great. Now Dan's colleague was suspecting him of domestic abuse.

'It was my idea,' I said.

'It's all right, you don't have to –'

'Yes, I do. I don't want anyone getting the wrong idea. I asked Dan if he'd, er, do the necessary if things got out of hand. It all came from me. He wasn't even that keen on any of it.' I paused. 'To begin with.'

Patrick, the tips of his ears bright red, mumbled, 'Right.'

'So,' I continued, 'I was out of order tonight, having too much to drink so I couldn't drive home, so he gets to, y'know, deliver a bit of summary justice. Crime and punishment, that's your business, isn't it? Not hard to understand, I hope.'

Patrick considered this. 'Well, no,' he said. 'And not even any paperwork to fill in afterwards, eh, Dan?'

'Not for me,' he muttered, sounding slightly less stressed.

'It's different anyway,' said Patrick. 'Different strokes ...'

'Literally,' I said and he laughed, thawing.

'Well, that's given me something to think about,' he said. 'When I saw you two down there at first, I thought something else was going on. Especially when he lifted up your skirt. I thought I'd better get down and warn you, before you got done for indecent exposure. And then you started ... well, I couldn't stop watching. I wasn't sure I could believe my eyes. By the time I got down there, old Uniform was on the case. I know him, by the way, used to work at Sands Lane nick before he retired from the job. If you want me to have a word ...'

'I don't think that'll be necessary,' said Dan. 'I think he's let it go.'

'So,' said Patrick, turning into our street. 'If Dan winds you up, do you get to wallop his backside?'

I laughed again. 'It doesn't work that way.'

'Tch. I thought we were all about equality these days.'

'Yeah,' I said. 'And it's my equal right not to want to spank my husband. Besides, he's practically perfect in every way.'

I said it with a certain malicious glee, knowing that Dan had had the nickname 'Mary Poppins' when he joined the force as a somewhat over-eager young constable. It served him right after all that Twinkletoes stuff earlier.

Patrick laughed heartily at that as he parked up outside our block.

'Oh, well, all's forgotten and forgiven, I'm sure,' he said.

'Thanks for this, Pat,' said Dan, unbuckling his seat-belt. 'You won't say anything, will you? If this gets round the station ...'

'Don't worry, mate. Though it's a lovely juicy bit of gossip.' He sighed.

'Pat!'

'Don't worry. Night. Go on with you. Kiss and make up.'

'Thanks,' I whispered, making a quick getaway towards the communal door of the block.

Once inside, Dan sank down on to the sofa, put his head in his hands and moaned, 'Fuck.'

'It's OK,' I said. 'He won't say anything. D'you want coffee?'

'Please.'

He was less tense, though still pale, by the time I put the cup into his hands.

'Talk about a sobering experience,' he said.

'Yeah.' The two glasses of wine were a distant memory.

'I don't know what I was thinking. What a fucking

prat. Of course the car park had CCTV. Of course it did. Shit.'

'Dan, stop it. It doesn't matter. The concierge has probably forgotten all about it by now and Patrick promised not to say anything. It's fine. Let it go.'

'The concierge *and* Patrick are probably wanking *right now* to the memory of your bare arse over the car bonnet.' He put down the coffee and buried his head in his hands. 'Fuck,' he said again, drawing out the vowel sound in desperation.

'Don't beat yourself up about it. It was a silly mistake – everyone makes them from time to time. Even me.'

I hoped my little postscript would lighten his mood. If there's one thing I'd change about Dan, it's his tendency to agonise over every single little error.

'Pip, it's my job to exercise good judgement. I didn't exercise good judgement. I feel like my whole career is built on a lie.'

'Oh, for fuck's sake, get a grip,' I said, cross now. 'You'd had a few beers and you were a bit pissed off. And you were off-duty. It has nothing to do with your competence as a police officer. Please!'

'I should never have put us in that position. I could have been arrested. We both could have been arrested. We still could!'

'Dan.' I tried to speak very slowly and clearly, although my temper was riding up hard, snatching at the edges of my self-control. 'The concierge won't do anything. Patrick won't say anything. He might tease you a bit in the locker room, but that's as bad as it'll get. I'd swear to it. Can we please just forget it now?'

'I could have been charged with assault. It is assault, isn't it? Technically, it's actually assault, what I do to you.'

'Christ, if a bit of consensual spanking is assault, pity the poor bloody judges. The courts are going to be busting at the seams.'

Dan stopped angsting for a while and drank his coffee, staring out at the black night beyond the window.

'I really am sorry I had that second glass of wine,' I said. 'I wish I hadn't.'

'I don't know why you had the first.'

'There's never enough decent non-alcoholic stuff to drink at parties. I can't drink Coke all night. I'd never sleep.'

'That's a line of defence, if not a particularly stunning one.'

'I think you're turning this into a crisis when you don't need to. It isn't. It's a silly glitch, that's all. And you were only trying to do the right thing.'

'Yeah,' he said. 'But when I get mixed up with the right thing and the bloody stupid thing, perhaps it's time I accepted I'm not cut out for this.'

'Oh, really? What, for ...?'

'Domestic discipline,' he elucidated. 'To do it properly, I have to be, like, infallible. Don't I? I have to know what's best all the time. And I don't, Pip. I don't always know.' He wrung his hands, breathing fast, almost on the verge of tears. 'Sometimes I haven't got a fucking clue what I'm doing or why …'

I put down my coffee and flung my arms around him. He responded in kind and we held each other tight on the sofa while he worked at choking back his dismay.

'You don't have to be infallible,' I whispered, stroking his hair. 'You don't have to be perfect. That's your hang-up, darling, I know, but you really don't have to be this flawless individual.'

'I want to be,' he gasped. 'I wish I could be. For you.'

'I know, I know. You are, darling. You are perfect for me, because you try so hard and you make me so happy.'

'I get it wrong, though. I get things wrong.'

'We all get things wrong. We're human. We can't help it. I don't care if you don't always make the right call. I care that you're doing this for me because I asked you to and you love me and you want me to be happy. That's all that matters. Really and truly. All that matters. We love each other, don't we?'

'God, of course, of course we do.'

'So you don't have to be infallible. You don't have to be all-knowing. You just have to do what you do out of love. Just do that and it'll be all right. Always.'

He took a deep breath, recovering.

'You don't think I'm turning into a monster?' he asked.

'No!'

'You still think I'm sexy?'

I laughed, through a little haze of tears. 'You moron, of course I do. Because you are.'

He prodded my chest. 'Who are you calling a moron?'

I prodded his. 'You, sarge.'

'Come over here and say that.'

'I already am over here.'

'Oh, yeah. So you are.'

In a second he had me pinned to the sofa and screaming while he tickled the life out of me.

'Stop, stop,' I begged. 'Don't, I'd rather you spanked me than this!'

'Oh, yes?' He laid himself down on me, full-length, our noses tip to tip. 'I think I've had enough of that for one evening. But you might prefer this instead.'

His mouth covered mine, robbing the breath from my body. We writhed together, legs twisting around legs, hands in hair, pelvises grinding while we kissed and kissed until our lips were sore.

At one point we rolled together off the sofa and on to the rug, knocking the half-full coffee cups off the table, but for once Dan didn't fret about the stain.

Instead he picked me up and carried me into the bedroom. Our clothes came off slowly, the removal of

157

each garment interspersed with much more kissing and touching and linking of limbs. Once we were naked, he slid into me without meeting any resistance and we took it slowly, revelling in each thrust, each bump, each new burst of sensation. We didn't look away from each other once and we still kept eye contact when the slow build of pleasure crested into orgasm. I loved him so much I thought I might die of it. I know it sounds mushy and lame, but it's true, and I know he felt it too.

I wanted to feel his heart beating against mine for ever.

30 August

I left him snoring in bed when I went to work the next day, and he was on a night shift so I didn't see him when I got in.

A lot of the kids had had their GCSE results while I was on holiday, and work was frantic with discussions about their next steps, phone calls to local schools and colleges, helping with CVs and job applications. Last night's débâcle and its aftermath didn't have time to muscle into my consciousness until I got home.

Even then, it seemed like a storm in a teacup, but I texted Dan a smoochy little love note all the same, in case he was still het up about it.

He texted back, 'Just you wait till I get home,' which

made me smile and think that perhaps he was over his mini-crisis.

Of course, he didn't get home until I was grabbing my handbag and swallowing down the last of my toast, on the way out, so I was glad I hadn't waited but had simply gone to bed at the usual time and got a good night's sleep.

Tonight might be interesting though, I thought ...

And it was.

I got home at seven after an exhausting day and a trip to the clinic to get a morning-after pill for one of the girls who regularly attended the centre.

I knew Dan would be home, but there was no TV or radio noise, no clatter of pans in the kitchen. In fact, the flat was silent. Perhaps he was asleep?

I stuck my head around the living-room door – no sign, nor further in behind the kitchen partition.

The bathroom door was open, so he couldn't be in there. There only remained one place to look.

I opened the bedroom door slowly.

'Dan?' I whispered, in case he was asleep.

There was nobody in there. I walked further in, then screamed as he leapt out from behind the door and grabbed hold of me.

'What the fuck?' I shouted, adrenalin capering around my body like an acrobat.

He laughed and laughed.

'I'm sorry, I'm sorry, I couldn't resist it, oh, God, your face. Oh, come on. I'm sorry.' He pulled my resisting form into his arms and held me until I was still.

I noticed that he was wearing his uniform.

'What's with the new look? Are you moonlighting as a kissogram?'

He sat me down on the edge of the bed.

'No. Just thought it might add to the sense of occasion.'

'Have you got handcuffs?'

He patted his utility belt. It clinked.

'Oh, yes.'

'When you say "sense of occasion", you mean …?'

'I mean you can strip down to your underwear and put yourself in that corner over there until I'm ready for you.'

What was this? He'd gone from funny and flirty to Sergeant Authority in the blink of an eye. I felt like one of his suspects, collared for flicking him the Vs in the shopping centre – a silly kid who needed to be taught a lesson.

And because I was being spoken to like a rebellious fourteen-year-old, I found myself behaving like one.

'What for? I don't wanna.'

'Philippa, you can strip yourself or I can do it for you. Either way, you'll do as you're told.'

The words went straight between my thighs, making

me squirm and idly contemplate getting arrested by him some day. I wondered if his suspects ever felt turned on by his air of quiet assertiveness. Perhaps there were women who deliberately committed crimes, just to get cuffed by him. Mmm.

All the same, I felt like shouting that I knew my rights and I wanted my lawyer.

I was pouting as I took off my work clothes, and I flung them gracelessly to the floor, refusing to look at him.

'Laundry basket,' he said with a sigh.

Standing there with his arms folded and his shirt so white and his trousers so black, he seemed to tower over me, a presence to inspire fear and awe.

I dumped the clothes in the basket and stood there for longer than necessary, staring into the crumpled swirls of fabric, unwilling or unable to make my own way to the corner.

'That's the first half of the order,' said Dan. 'Can you remember the second?'

I humphed and did a hostile little shrug.

'I think you can. Go on.'

'I don't want to stand in the corner. I'd rather just get it over with.'

'I'd rather not have to deal with insubordination during discipline, Philippa. If you want extra punishment, you're going about it very well.'

I stamped my foot and dawdled over to the corner. Damn, he was so uncompromising when he was in this mood. And so sexy, I thought, stealing a furtive glance from the corner of my eye.

I wanted to smile, then. After all, this was what I wanted. And yet I still felt I ought to resist, I ought to protest. I ought to fight for the dignity I had willingly relinquished. It was stupid, but I'm human, and humans are stupid.

I stood in the corner in my knickers and bra and folded my arms mutinously.

He came up to my shoulder and I heard the rattle of the cuffs before I felt his hand close over my upper arms and wrench them apart. He put my hands behind my back and cuffed them. Proper cuffs, these, not the type you get from the Ann Summers catalogue. Heavy, cold metal, weighing on your wrists until they ache. He locked them shut then patted my hip before withdrawing.

'I'll call you when I'm ready,' he said. 'If you move out of that corner, I'll put you straight back, with a plug inside you. Understood?'

I shivered, exquisitely captive. 'Yes, Sir.'

'Good. While you're there, I want you to think about the perils of drinking and driving.'

'I didn't drink and drive, Sir.'

'No, I know, but I still want you to think about it.'

He left the room.

I have to confess, I didn't think about drink driving for one minute. I thought about my poor bottom and what might be about to happen to it. I clenched my cheeks and imagined the sound of the cane swishing through the air towards me. I didn't think I could take it.

I also thought about the feel of the cuffs on my wrists, how they contained and constrained me and restricted what I could do. I liked the feeling, despite the discomfort. I liked the idea that Dan could modify my behaviour, just as these cuffs modified my potential for physical move-ment. I liked the feeling of benign imprisonment, of it all being for my own good, because he cared about me.

I thought about the butt plug and how it had felt, and how it might feel if he put it in me now. He'd said he was going to keep them for after spankings. Would he do that tonight? Something about the plug reminded me at the deepest, basest level that I had submitted myself to him. I could carry on fooling myself through anything else, but the plug left no room for self-delusion. The plug told the truth of the matter.

Again, I clenched my buttocks. My legs were feeling a little trembly now. I pushed my nose right into the corner and made condensation on the paintwork with my breath until he opened the door again.

'Have you had time to think about why you're being punished tonight?' he asked.

'I don't need time to think about that. I already know.'

My adolescent-style whining was really coming to the fore tonight.

'You do? So, are you going to tell me?'

'Because I had too much to drink and couldn't drive home. And because ...' I stopped. I really wanted to say, 'because you want to', but at the last minute my bravado failed me.

'Because?'

'No other reason. Just that.'

'I see. And have you considered the reason you drank too much? Was it simply forgetfulness or a moment of madness?'

Ah. OK. Now he was asking. Because of course it wasn't either of those.

'No,' I said quietly.

'So what was it?'

'I was annoyed.'

'Annoyed why?'

'With you. Because I wanted to leave and you wanted to stay.'

'Right. So you drank too much to drive home as a way of getting your own back on me.'

'I was bored.'

'So, boredom and passive aggression?'

I sighed heavily.

'You see, it's fine for me to take you to your friends'

parties and sit there drinking lemonade and being looked daggers at and whispered about. But it's not fine for you to be bored for an hour while my friends do their best to entertain you.'

Gah. When he put it that way, it did make me sound like a bit of a brat. I couldn't stand that he had a point. I didn't want to acknowledge it. But I had to.

'I'm sorry,' I muttered.

'I didn't catch that.'

'I'm sorry,' I said, not in a particularly apologetic manner.

'Are you really? That sounded like it came from a very grudging place. Let's see how grudging you are with your apologies when we're done here, shall we?'

'No, I really am,' I said, twisting around from my corner position and turning on the beseeching eyes.

'Here,' he said, and he picked up two pillows and put them into the middle of the bed. 'Come and put yourself over these.'

'What are you going to do?' I asked, approaching dubiously.

'I'm going to do what you want me to do,' he said.

How could such words be so ominous?

I swallowed and shuffled forwards. It was surprisingly difficult to maintain balance with heavy metal cuffs on my wrists. I knelt on the bed and wriggled myself into position. The time for argument was past. I just had to take my medicine and hope it wasn't too foul.

'You aren't going to use the cane, are you?' I blurted. 'Please.'

I heard his heavy police-issue boots on the wooden floor, moving from one side of me to the other. He sat and put his hand on my cotton-clad bottom.

'I don't think you deserve the cane for this,' he said, more kindly than before. 'If you'd tried to drive the car without telling me you'd had too much wine, then yes, most definitely, I'd have called that a caning offence. But you were honest when it counted, so I'll leave it in the cupboard for tonight.'

I exhaled hugely.

Now that was out of the way, I thought I might even be looking forward to my punishment.

'Thanks,' I said meekly.

'You're welcome,' he said, with two heavy pats on my bum, not exactly spanks but not far off.

He stood up again and went to get something from another room.

Lying on my front over the pillows, handcuffed, with my face in the duvet, it wasn't easy to look around and see what was going on. I had to twist my neck into uncomfortable contortions to see the door. I decided to keep my head down and try to be zen about the whole thing. What would be would be; there was no point anticipating or fighting it.

When he came back again, he put what felt like an

167

armful of things down on the bed by my feet. He knelt behind me, lifted my hips and reached underneath to add another pillow, obviously thinking my bum wasn't sticking out enough. Now it was pushed up high, my cotton knickers straining over my cheeks. The spanking was going to hurt.

But I was at least allowed to keep my knickers on, which was a good sign. At least, I thought so.

He picked something up and I wondered if it was a paddle or a strap or something completely different.

It was something completely different.

It was a bath sponge.

I squealed and then giggled as drops of cold water fell like heavy rain on to my bum and soaked into my knickers.

'Oh, my God, what?' I exclaimed.

'Keep still.' He pushed my cuffed hands into the small of my back, away from the waterfall. The trickle continued to drip all over my cheeks, sinking in, slowly but surely, until I was wearing a pair of thoroughly wet panties, right down to the crotch. The coldness made me shiver.

'It's freezing,' I complained.

'Not for long,' he said.

One loud, wet smack fell hard on my bottom.

'Christ!'

It hurt. It hurt more than it did on dry bare flesh.

Something about the water added an element of fierce sting to proceedings.

'Painful?' asked Dan sternly.

'Very.'

'So it should be.'

He added another dozen smacks, hard and fast, while I gritted my teeth and tried hard to be brave. Once he had delivered twenty or so, he stopped and warned me that he was going to move on to the strap.

'It hurts,' I wailed.

'I know. Twenty strokes.'

The feeling of that leather falling like vengeance on my poor wet bum was something I couldn't have imagined. It stung like a swarm of bees, the smart spreading outwards and chasing away the cold. My knickers clung to my bottom as if glued, the strokes making loud slappy sounds each time the strap fell.

'It really hurts,' I shouted. 'More than anything.'

I tried to reach down with my cuffed hands, to protect my bottom from the onslaught, but I knew it would make no difference, so I had to content myself with trying to twist away from the strap. He put his hand on my back and held me in position and carried on regardless.

I lost count early on, too busy kicking and gasping to try anything more mentally challenging.

'My goodness, this is certainly very effective,' he said, laying them on with inexorable force. 'I'll remember this.'

169

I tried a sobbing noise, to see if it would stop him. It didn't.

I suppose he must have gone past the dozen mark by the time I decided I'd do anything to end this.

'Dan, I can't!' I shouted. 'It's too much.'

He stopped straight away and crouched over me, his hand rubbing my spine.

'OK, OK, love,' he said. 'Do you want me to stop completely or do you just need a break?'

I thought about this. If I wanted to, I could wriggle out of the rest of the punishment. It was a tempting prospect, but I knew that, if I succumbed to the temptation, I'd feel weirdly disappointed. I didn't want Dan to let me off, just as I got indignant on his behalf when crooks he'd arrested got away scot-free or with a light sentence. Having been fairly tried and convicted, I didn't want to dodge any of my punishment. And I didn't want to feel that I could manipulate Dan any time I wanted either. I wanted to know that I was going to get what he thought I deserved. I needed him to have that strength and focus. He thought I should get twenty with the strap, so I wanted twenty with the strap. The wet-bottom thing was a bit much, though, all the same.

But I needed to show him that I had faith in him.

So I lifted my head, stuck my bum back out and said, 'No, I'm OK. Just needed to catch my breath.'

'You're quite something, you know?' he said softly, then he picked the strap back up. 'Sure?'

I nodded.

'Right. Seven more, and they're going to be hard.'

Fine. As long as you don't put any more of that water on me.

The first stroke was a blast of shocking pain and I cursed myself for not getting out when I had the chance. Jeez, what an idiot. But I was determined to be strong and, although I yelled out, I kept myself in position.

I keened through the next few until, with only three left to go, he decided to lower my damp knickers and finish off on my damp bare bottom.

This added an extra heat and a sharp edge. It was almost unbearable. Almost. But I bore it.

After the twentieth and final stroke, I let down my guard and began to cry. My bottom hurt like mad but I felt absurdly happy and light – a kind of unburdening, I suppose.

Dan sat beside me and rubbed my shoulders and whispered soothing words.

'I love you, Pip,' he said. 'Don't ever think I don't love you.'

'I know,' I wept. 'That's why I'm crying. Because you love me enough to do this. It's happy tears.'

He lay down and pulled me on to him – it was pretty difficult with my hands cuffed, and it took a few minutes to get into a comfortable position, but eventually I lay with my cheek on his shoulder, held in his arms.

'I just want to kiss and make up now,' he said. 'Make it all better for you. Run you a bath and rub some lotion into your bum. But I promised myself I wouldn't do that yet.'

'No? Why not? What are you going to do instead?'

'I'm going to pay you back for that Mary Poppins comment.'

I craned my neck to catch his eye.

'That was to pay *you* back for the Twinkletoes comment.'

'Don't care. I'm going to get my revenge and there's nothing you can do about it because you're wearing handcuffs.'

'That's not fair!'

'Awww.' He ruffled my hair. 'I know. But I am the law.'

He slid out from underneath me, leaving me prone on the duvet, jerking about like a wet fish in my efforts to raise myself up.

'Dan, I can't take any more of that strap,' I warned him.

'Who said anything about spanking?'

I tried to look at him, but my neck threatened to crick so I buried my face back in the plump, soft cotton.

'You can get back over those pillows, though. Here, let me give you a hand. Since you don't have the use of yours.'

He helpfully shoved the three pillows back under my stomach, arching me over with my bum uppermost again.

'Let's have these a bit wider, shall we?' he suggested, nudging my thighs apart with his palms.

'What are you going to do?' I asked nervously. 'Is it going to hurt?'

'No. Well, I hope not. Maybe a little.'

I knew then what he was going to do. At least, I thought I did, but when I heard a quiet buzzing behind me I decided I must be wrong.

The vibrator felt cold against my inner thigh, but it soon warmed on its travels up and down both legs. By the time it arrived between my pussy lips, I was ready for it. I sighed with satisfaction when Dan stroked it around my clit, occasionally pressing it down against the swollen bud. This was lovely. All my tension was floating away, replaced by sheer pleasure.

'Oh, that's nice,' I murmured.

'I'm good to you, aren't I?' he said, switching the vibe up a gear. Now waves of stronger arousal pulsed through me. I longed for him to really rub hard at my clit, but he kept easing off when things seemed to be building to a head.

'You're good ... oh ... please ...' If this was revenge, he was serving it very hot. Stupid proverbs, what do they know?

Just at the point before the point of no return, he took

the vibrator away from my clit, causing me to buck my hips in a wild physical protest. He waited until I was still, then fed the length of juddering plastic into my vagina, inch by slow inch.

I wanted him to touch my clitoris. I was so close, so close to a spectacular orgasm, fuelled by my hot, sore bottom. But he didn't touch my clit and, once the vibrator was halfway in, he pulled it back out again, then inserted just the final inch, leaving it buzzing away there for such a long time that I eventually snapped in frustration.

'For God's sake, Dan, just fuck me.'

'Ooh, temper,' he goaded, taking the vibrator out again.

'Please,' I wheedled, shimmying my hips.

'Well, I might just do that,' he said, filling my pussy with vibrations once more. 'But be careful what you wish for, love. Because it might not be quite what you expect.'

I was right, I was right. I knew what he was preparing for.

The first lubed-up fingertip between my cheeks felt like a vindication. It also felt extremely rude and a little bit frightening, even though he had done this several times before, when using the plugs. But this time I knew there would be no plug.

He began to work the finger firmly towards my rear entrance. The curious helplessness of my arms was both troubling and reassuring. It saved me having to put up the token fight. All I had to do was lie there and take it.

'Are you going to …?'

'What do you think, love?'

'You are.'

'I am.'

His fingertip twisted and prodded, making me yield a little bit of ground with each determined probe. Soon he would have me open and ready for him. Soon I would know how that felt. And all the while, the vibrator kept up its low level stimulation, holding me on its high-tension wire.

I made a short, sharp exclamation as the finger popped through the tight ring and dug inside.

'Got you,' he whispered. 'Right where I want you. Shall we speed this up, hmm?'

The vibrator's shakings intensified.

I groaned with the strange … well, was it pleasure? I didn't know. It was *something* but I couldn't quite identify it … of having both holes occupied. I felt as if everything of me was concentrated in that low pit of sensation. Arms, legs, brain, all useless. I was nothing but cunt and arse, nothing but sex. It was all I was good for.

Dan's finger speared up further, settling into an aggressive rhythm. It didn't hurt but it felt wriggly and made my stomach release butterflies.

'I want to put my cock up there,' he said. 'I want to fuck your arse.'

'I know,' I said, my voice coming out in sympathy with the vibrator, low and shuddery.

'You want me to. You want my cock right here.' He jabbed with the enclosed finger.

'Yeah, yeah,' I said in short gasps.

'Good. Right. Settle down there, then.'

He took out his finger and let more cold lube drip between my cheeks from a height. I heard him taking off his belt and his trousers and his boots.

I wriggled and clamped my thighs, trying to find the perfect spot of friction on the vibrator.

'Keep still,' he ordered.

But it was hard, very hard to keep still. I was desperate to introduce the vibrator to my G-spot, so I could melt into a big gooey mess on the duvet. I knew that would disappoint Dan, who was now in a frenzy of lustful anticipation, so I tried to focus my mind on the spot of bedroom wall that needed replastering and forget that I was stuffed full of vibrator, awaiting sodomisation.

His hands felt big and authoritative on my bum cheeks, pulling them wide. I knew he was kneeling behind me. I knew what was coming.

'OK, OK,' he said, to himself, it seemed. Perhaps he was trying to hold himself steady. 'Slowly.'

Something long and warm and thick placed itself in

the crease of my bottom, rubbing up and down, spreading the lubricant all around. How would it compare to the plug? I wondered if it would be thicker. It was certainly longer.

The rounded tip of it butted my opening and I knew straight away that this part of it would not go in as easily as the tapered end of the plug.

I had to work at not clenching or trying to derail him. He took hold of a hip and pulled it towards him, easing forward.

'I think I'm going to have to give it one good thrust, love,' he said. 'Or I'm going to dither here for too long. Hold tight.'

The lube eased his passage and he slipped in speedily, if a little eye-wateringly. God, he felt big. Really big, much bigger than the plug.

I couldn't help myself; I closed my muscles against him, trying to repel the invasion.

But he only groaned and forged forward.

'God, you're so tight, oh, God. Fuck.'

The weight of delight in his voice allayed my little outburst of panic. He was slap-bang in the middle of a moment he'd fantasised about for a long time. I wasn't going to take that away from him, even if it did sting like he'd rubbed raw chilli on his cock.

And the sting didn't last, anyway. It was already dying down, to be replaced by a throb, a sort of dull ache. He was big and he was stretching me – I was going to be aware of this throughout. There was no way around it.

He made one last push and that was as far as he could go.

'This is just ...' He groaned. 'Your arse is hot and you feel so ... oh, God. I'm sorry, I can't ... I'm so close already.'

'It's OK,' I whispered.

'Not OK, too soon. Got to ... think of crime stats ... housebreaking down 14 per cent, violent assaults went up over the summer months ... right.'

His breathing steadied and he held himself perfectly still.

'Does it hurt?' he whispered.

'A bit. Not much.'

'I'll take it easy.'

I don't think he could have taken it easier, but I still found it the most squirm-inducing experience of my life. To feel that pressure and that friction and that *movement*. I mean, I'd had the first element with the plug, but the last two, no, that was new. I couldn't help tightening around him, in my body's mistaken assumption that this would expel its intruder, instead of holding him even closer.

He sawed slowly back and forth, and then, after a while, he remembered the dildo and he put his hand down there and began to jiggle it. It made me feel impossibly full, almost as if my entire lower body had been reconfigured. I no longer knew what was going where, what was thrusting and what was screwing.

All I could do was shut my eyes and take it.

The constant burn didn't stop the pleasure from building. At first it was centred inside my pussy, then it seemed to spread outwards, to tap into my bottom, to swish around the top of my legs and the pit of my stomach.

At last it inhabited me entirely and I was its creature. My orgasm wrenched me out of everything controllable and took hold of me, a bodysnatcher.

Dan pumped harder, whispering, 'Oh, yeah, oh, yeah, you like this, take this,' until he emptied himself inside me and pushed me down flat on the bed, crushing me to the mattress.

I shed a few tears, nothing to do with pain or sadness, everything to do with exhaustion and intensity. He pushed his cheek against mine and turned his face to kiss me.

'Are you OK? Was that all right? You should have said if I ...'

'No, no, it was good. Surprisingly. Powerful.'

'You're sure?'

'Positive.'

We fell asleep like that and I dreamt I was trapped by an avalanche.

25 December

I know, I know.

It's been months since I last updated. I meant to keep this more regularly, but it's been a busy time. Besides, I have that *other* diary to keep now. Dan's famous online discipline journal. He makes me write in it every day, and describe the day and what I've found difficult and what I'm getting better at. If I've earned a punishment, he makes me blog about it in fine detail – pseudonymously, of course. Then he adds his comments and sends it out into the web for general perusal.

It's weird, but we've made a lot of new friends through it. At first, I was terrified we'd out ourselves, but we're careful and at first nobody seemed to read it anyway, much to my relief.

But then, as autumn crept towards winter, we started to get comments. And the commenters linked us on their own blogs. And then we got more comments and more links until we seem to have become part of a big online community of corporal-punishment enthusiasts. Some are more extreme than us, and some have an ideological stance we don't agree with, whilst some are at the milder end of the scale, but we're all in a similar boat – some of us sitting less comfortably than others.

At first I was horribly embarrassed by this, but now it's nice to have friends who are in a similar position, striving for the same things. I've had lots of good advice, and so has Dan, and it's kept us going even when we've started to feel discouraged or freakish for what we do.

As far as I know, my old university friends still think I walk all over Dan's back in pointy stilettos. As for Dan's colleagues at the station, I don't think Patrick has said anything to them, although he makes the odd snide remark in the locker room from time to time.

Work continues to be fraught and stressful and, while I still snap and bitch at Dan when I come home after a particularly shitty day, the inevitable bottom-warming that follows heads off the moody sulks I used to indulge in and clears the air.

And it relieves some of his stress too. Win win.

We even met up with a couple we got to know through our blog. I wasn't keen on this – it seemed too soon. But emails flew between us and eventually they talked us round. We went for a drink in town and they were lovely – slightly older than us, but they'd been living this 'lifestyle' since they met and were very experienced.

I stood outside the pub for ages, telling Dan I didn't think I could go through with it. I didn't think I could look them in the eye, knowing what they knew about me.

'We don't have to do this, Pip, but we can't just stand them up. Let's go inside and say you aren't feeling well.'

'They'll try to reschedule,' I wailed, taking a few steps away towards the tube station.

Dan took a firm hold of my wrist and shook his head.

'Don't run away from me,' he said. 'It's basic good manners to apologise to them. Come on.'

'Well, if I have to face them anyway, I might as well stay. I don't want to go in there. Dan. Don't make me.'

'You're being ridiculous, Philippa.'

Uh oh. Philippa. Code for 'I am considering spanking you'.

And then a woman came out of the pub and said, 'It *is* you, isn't it?' and I couldn't make my excuse after all.

It was excruciating at first, having their eyes on me, feeling that they knew my deepest secrets. They knew all about the caning and how I howled my head off and locked myself in the bathroom. They knew about the time Dan put ginger root up my bum and it burned so that I couldn't keep still. Worst of all, they knew all about my silly little foibles and shamefully childish strops.

But after ten minutes the mortification began to ease. Or maybe that was the wine. (I wasn't driving.) Plus, for everything they knew about me, I knew all about them. I knew that Prissy (which is what the wife called herself – still don't know her real name) was punished for obsessive-compulsive behaviour as a kind of therapy, as well as for missing meals. She was a recovering anorexic, and she was recovering well, looking healthy and happy and full of the joys. She credited domestic discipline with saving her marriage, her sanity and her life. I was impressed.

'It's not that big a deal for me,' I said, 'but it's certainly smoothed out a few rough corners in our relationship. Now I'm less grumpy and Dan's less anxious and we're both a lot closer, I think.'

Prissy and I paired off while Dan and her husband ('Slowhand') did the same and then, after a couple more drinks, we merged back into the original quartet.

Slowhand asked Dan if he'd ever considered punishing me in front of anyone else and I began to bristle, thinking that invitations to swing weren't far off. He shook his head, though, and said it was private and he wouldn't want to do anything I was too uncomfortable with.

'Dan's the only man I'll ever let near my bare bum,' I said. 'Ever.'

And they left it at that.

It's nice to have friends in the 'community' though and, while that particular aspect isn't for us, I think a lot of our online contacts enjoy a 'spanking party' now and again.

So that's my update.

And now it's Christmas Day, and the best one ever.

We're at my parents' house in the spare room, and Dan is still downstairs watching some crappy film with a mince pie and the last of several festively flavoured brandies. It's the first year since we married that he hasn't had to be on duty for at least some part of the holidays, and we're making the most of it, before he has to go back and do the whole of the New Year.

I've crept up for a bit of peace and quiet and because I hate shoot-'em-up movies and ... well ... I'm feeling reflective.

Literally reflective, because as soon as I got up here, I went to the wardrobe mirror and lifted up my dress and had a look at my bottom. It's still a tiny bit red and there are bruises here and there.

I'm on Santa's Naughty List this year.

We spent Christmas morning at home before driving up here for lunch and I had some interesting stocking fillers. Dan made me look in my stocking before I could even give him his Christmas blowjob. I woke him up with a snog and a 'Merry Christmas' and I was slithering down his stomach, kissing all the way, when he put his hand in my hair and said, 'No, not yet.'

'But it's traditional,' I said, wide-eyed. 'If we're together on Christmas morning we have … breakfast in bed …'

'We can still do that,' he said. 'But I want you to go into the living room and see what's in your stocking.'

'Oh.' I began to see the way things might be going. 'Santa's been to the adult shops this year? Or did he get the elves to make them? Poor corrupted elves.'

'Go and see.' He gave my bottom a smack.

I jumped, naked, out of the bed and hotfooted it to the living room. My stocking hung, as usual, on the corner of the mantelpiece. Something was protruding from the top, the handle of something tied with red and green ribbon.

I dipped in my hand and brought out a supple leather riding crop. It looked and smelled expensive – a proper one from a tack shop, not a cheapy X-rated special.

Why did Dan think this would make a good present? I didn't have a horse and I didn't like riding … oh.

I was the horse. I was the one getting ridden.

I put it down and delved further. Tiny thong knickers in bright red velvet with white marabou trimming. How festive. I put them on; they barely covered anything. Then there were red sequinned pasties with beaded tassels to put on my nipples – this wasn't easy as I had to get the suction right but I managed in the end. A headband with little fuzzy antlers was easy enough to work out, but what was this?

The final ingredient was a butt plug – a butt plug with a plaited horsehair tail attached. It seemed I was coming as Rudolph. Rude-olph.

I stuck the antler hair-band on and marched into the bedroom, brandishing the plug.

'Is this your idea of festive?' I said, pouting, and he laughed uproariously.

'Yes,' he said. 'Totally. And you look gorgeous, but your outfit's missing something. Get the lube and bring it over here.'

'I'm not wearing a butt plug on Christmas Day!'

'Yes, you are,' he said, brooking no argument. 'Get the lube.'

I had to fight the smile off my face but I managed somehow to turn it into a heavy frown and I took the lubricant bottle from my bedside cupboard and thrust it at him.

'You can do this, can't you?' he said. 'Put it in. I'll hold the thong out of the way for you. Kneel in front of me.'

'You're horrible,' I moaned, but I did as I was told, because I was quite excited by then.

I greased up the plug and reached around, straining to push it as easily as I could into my bottom. I'd done this a few times now and I knew it wasn't impossible, but this plug was quite large and I had to huff and puff a bit and pull it out and try again a fair few times.

Dan held the thong aside patiently, uttering words of encouragement.

'That's it. Push. Get it in. Does that burn, love? Like it does when I fuck you there? That's good, now you're my little red-nosed reindeer. Without the red nose.'

I had a feeling something else might be red before he was finished with me.

'OK,' he said, 'hands and knees, on the floor. Make your way back into the living room.'

I crawled along, Dan at my heels, until I reached the sofa on which I had thrown the riding crop.

'Ah, here it is,' he said, picking it up and holding it close to my face. 'What do you think?'

'Weird kind of Christmas present,' I grumbled.

'You might think so. But I've been dreaming of a red hot Christmas.'

'Christmarse,' I said.

'Smart arse.' He sliced the crop down on my bottom. It hurt a lot.

'Ouch!' I rubbed the affected area.

'I like the idea of you sitting uncomfortably while you eat your turkey. I like it a lot.'

He began to beat a swift tattoo with the crop on my poor defenceless bottom while I bent forward and yowled into the cushions. That thing created a blaze in no time.

187

I writhed and moaned but he gave me a good thirty solid strokes, all over my bottom and thighs, until I thought my skin was so tight it might burst.

'You're so mean,' I howled, once he had put the thing down.

'Tell me you don't love it,' he challenged.

Of course, I couldn't.

'It hurts,' I prevaricated.

'Of course it does. But that doesn't mean you don't love it, does it?'

I maintained a sulky silence, but only until he lowered his pyjama trousers and pushed, swiftly and surprisingly, into me from behind. The little plaited tail of the butt plug got wedged between his pelvis and my sore bottom as he thrust, creating an extra element of friction that I quite enjoyed. I also pushed back against him, revelling in the slap of his skin against my hot, aching bum and the way his cock jiggled the plug each time he plunged in.

'Merry ... Christmas ...' he panted. He curled two fingers between my soaked pussy lips, just in time for me to crash into a mighty climax.

He followed suit, clutching at the butt-plug tail, rolling his hips against my curved cheeks.

We slumped against the sofa together, hot, sticky bodies entwined.

'What about your Christmas blowjob?' I protested. 'I don't suppose you'll want that now.'

'Sometimes traditions can get a bit stale,' he said, yawning. 'It's good to freshen up the routine.'

'Yeah,' I said. 'Cream instead of brandy butter. White lights on the tree instead of multicoloured. Hot sex dressed as a reindeer instead of a blowjob. Shall I send that tip in to the festive style magazines?'

'Yeah.'

'Don't fall asleep on me,' I said, alarmed, as his full weight pinned me to the sofa. 'We've got to be at Mum and Dad's for half twelve, remember. We need to shower, dress, breakfast, remove butt plug, all the usual morning stuff.'

'Think you should keep it in,' he slurred, but he didn't mean it. Thank God.

Christmas dinner with butt plug firmly ensconced would not have been fun. It was bad enough having to shift around on my seat to find the least bruised spot to perch on while I helped myself to stuffing and bread sauce. I usually wore a little black dress on Christmas Day, but this time I stuck to a safe trousers-and-sparkly-top combo. Didn't want any accidental up-the-skirt eyefuls.

Dan had a knowing glint in his eye throughout the meal. He kept asking me if I was sitting comfortably, the git. Luckily, everyone else was oblivious. Everyone, that is, except Weird Great-Uncle Colin, who, despite his tendency to fall asleep halfway through dinner, is like an innuendo-seeking missile.

'Still working with your difficult young 'uns, are you, Pip?' he asked, necking back his third sherry.

'That's right,' I confirmed. 'They're not all difficult, you know. Most of them want to live good lives. They just don't know how.'

'Hmm, well, I know what I'd do with 'em,' he said. 'Bring back the birch. Thrash the lot of 'em. That'd put all the drugs and gangs nonsense out of their heads all right.'

I shook my head, preparing my defence, but Dan nipped in before me.

'Really, Colin?' he asked, as if hanging on the man's every word. 'You think corporal punishment is effective?'

I kicked him under the table. In the process, a particularly painful area of my bottom made contact with the chair frame. Ouch.

'I know so,' he said. 'Works wonders. All those ne'er-do-wells you must pick up every day of the week for … throwing stones and painting on walls. Don't you wish you could just give 'em a good hiding instead of a caution? What bloody good's a caution, eh? You've been a bad boy, don't do it again. They *do* do it again. Don't they? Eh?'

'Many of them do, yes,' admitted Dan. 'And it is frustrating to see people given ASBOs which they break time and again, with no negative consequences for them.

All the same, I wouldn't want to go back to hanging and flogging. Not for kids.'

At 'not for kids', Uncle Colin's ears pricked up and I felt a wave of heat plunge from my cheeks downwards. *Shut up, Dan.*

'No? So who would you hang and flog then, if not kids?'

I pushed my plate away.

'Blimey, I'm absolutely stuffed,' I said. 'Better take a break before pudding.'

'I wouldn't *hang* anyone,' said Dan. He looked at me, lip curving upwards.

'I'll take out the empty plates, shall I?'

It was a relief to stand up, and even more of a relief to get out of the room and into the still of the kitchen.

Dan came in a few minutes later and stood behind me, his hands clasped around my waist, while I dealt with the leftovers.

'Awkward,' he said with a chuckle.

'I thought you were going to give the game away then,' I whispered.

'Game? Is it a game?'

I looked up at him, at his earnest brow and his serious eyes. It was the first Christmas Day ever without a stress-related tiff.

'No,' I said. 'It's not a game.'

And it isn't.

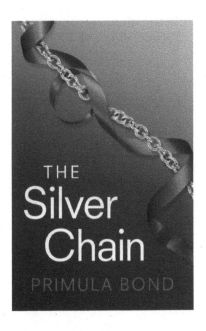

THE SILVER CHAIN – PRIMULA BOND

Good things come to those who wait…

After a chance meeting one evening, mysterious entrepreneur Gustav Levi and photographer Serena Folkes agree to a very special contract.

Gustav will launch Serena's photographic career at his gallery, but only if Serena agrees to become his companion.

To mark their agreement, Gustav gives Serena a bracelet and silver chain which binds them physically and symbolically. A sign that Serena is under Gustav's power.

As their passionate relationship intensifies, the silver chain pulls them closer together. But will Gustav's past tear them apart?

A passionate, unforgettable erotic romance for fans of *50 Shades of Grey* and Sylvia Day's *Crossfire Trilogy*.

GAME – JUSTINE ELYOT

The stakes are high, the game is on.

In this sequel to Justine Elyot's bestselling *On Demand*, Sophie discovers a whole new world of daring sexual exploits.

Sophie's sexual tastes have always been a bit on the wild side – something her boyfriend Lloyd has always loved about her.

But Sophie gives Lloyd every part of her body except her heart. To win all of her, Lloyd challenges Sophie to live out her secret fantasies.

As the game intensifies, she experiments with all kinds of kinks and fetishes in a bid understand what she really wants. But Lloyd feature in her final decision? Or will the ultimate risk he takes drive her away from him?

Find out more at www.mischiefbooks.com

POWER PLAY – CHARLOTTE STEIN

Now she's the boss, everything that once seemed forbidden is possible…

Meet Eleanor Harding, a woman who loves to be in control and who puts Anastasia Steele in the shade.

When Eleanor is promoted, she loses two very important things: the heated relationship she had with her boss, and control over her own desires.

She finds herself suddenly craving something very different – and office junior, Ben, seems like just the sort of man to fulfil her needs. He's willing to show her all of the things she's been missing – namely, what it's like to be the one in charge.

Now all Eleanor has to do is decide…is Ben calling the kinky shots, or is she?

Find out more at www.mischiefbooks.com

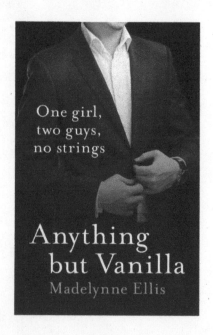

ANYTHING BUT VANILLA
MADELYNNE ELLIS

One girl, two guys, no strings.

Kara North is on the run. Fleeing from her controlling fiancé and a wedding she never wanted, she accepts the chance offer of refuge on Liddell Island, where she soon catches the eye of the island's owner, erotic photographer Ric Liddell.

But pleasure comes in more than one flavour when Zachary Blackwater, the charming ice-cream vendor also takes an interest, and wants more than just a tumble in the surf.

When Kara learns that the two men have been unlikely lovers for years, she becomes obsessed with the idea of a threesome.

Soon Kara is wondering how she ever considered committing herself to just one man.

Find out more at www.mischiefbooks.com